THE KAHLIL GIBRAN READER

KAHLIL GIBRAN READER

INSPIRATIONAL WRITINGS

Kahlil Gibran

A Birch Lane Press Book
Published by Carol Publishing Group

A Birch Lane Press Book
Published by Carol Publishing Group
Birch Lane Press is a registered trademark of Carol Communications, Inc.
Editorial Offices: 600 Madison Avenue, New York, N.Y. 10022
Sales & Distribution Offices: 120 Enterprise Avenue,
Secaucus, N.J. 07094
In Canada: Canadian Manda Group, One Atlantic Avenue,
Suite 105, Toronto, Ontario M6K 3E7
Queries regarding rights and permissions should be addressed to
Carol Publishing Group, 600 Madison Avenue, New York, N.Y. 10022

Carol Publishing Group books are available at special discounts for bulk purchases, sales promotions, fund-raising, or educational purposes. Special editions can be created to specifications.
For details contact: Special Sales Department,
Carol Publishing Group, 120 Enterprise Avenue,
Secaucus, N.J. 07094

Manufactured in the United States of America
10 9 8 7 6 5 4 3 2 1

Library of Congress Cataloging-in-Publication Data
Gibran, Kahlil, 1883–1931.
[Selections. English 1995]
The Kahlil Gibran reader : inspirational writings.—A special gift ed.
p. cm.
"Birch Lane Press book."
ISBN 1-55972-293-2
1. Gibran, Kahlil, 1883–1931—Translations into English.
I. Title.
PJ7826.I2 1995 94–44940
892'.715—dc20 CIP

Contents

Introduction

The immortal writings of Kahlil Gibran, the *Prophet of Lebanon,* possess a rare and distinctive flavor of ancient wisdom and mysticism that is equaled by few—if any—in the history of world literature. Small wonder, then, that the reader never ceases to be amazed at Gibran's recency to this world and age (1883–1931). The delicacy of his mind, the visions in his inner eyes, and the vast but simple insight displayed by his every parable combine to present a momentary incongruity. It is quickly dispelled, however, for one soon realizes that Gibran is of all ages.

The brilliance of Gibran will ever continue to surprise and perplex his millions of followers in dozens of languages. This strange man, born in the shadow of the Holy Cedars of Lebanon, exhibits a weirdly beautiful approach to life and death in all of his writings, never fully revealing the purpose behind his abrupt and intense changes in thought and style...from the laciest and tenderest language and meaning to the bitterest and angriest outpourings known to literature. After an attempted analysis that ended in utter dispair, a group of scholars at a leading university could only conclude, *Gibran could write timeless truths in a way that makes the reader feel he is taking a walk in a quiet wood, or bathing in a cool stream; it soothes the spirit. But he could also write with a scorch like fire.* The tremendous "why" could not be found.

Philosopher and artist, his dynamic brush is no less disturbing than his pen. The searching depths of mysticism, the unfettered glory of youth, and the Elysian beauty of death join forces to render his canvases remarkably fascinating and unique. As for his handling of materials and his artistry of representation, all that need be said is that when Auguste Rodin wished to have his own portrait done, he bypassed the multitude of accomplished and aspiring painters of his day and insisted that Gibran execute the project. Hundreds of Gibran's oil paintings are on permanent exhibit in a Lebanese museum erected solely as the repository for these works, and numerous of his paintings and drawings are displayed periodically in the large capitals and art centers of the world.

Gibran has a specific, recognizable message to convey, and the simplicity of his style—whether in delicacy or in bitter invective—brings that message to the inner consciousness of the reader quickly, clearly, and effortlessly.

MARTIN WOLF
New York City

THE KAHLIL GIBRAN READER

1

The Secrets of the Heart

A majestic mansion stood under the wings of the silent night, as Life stands under the cover of Death. In it sat a maiden at an ivory desk, leaning her beautiful head on her soft hand, as a withering lily leans upon its petals. She looked around, feeling like a miserable prisoner, struggling to penetrate the walls of the dungeon with her eyes in order to witness Life walking in the procession of Freedom.

The hours passed like the ghosts of the night, as a procession chanting the dirge of her sorrow, and the maiden felt secure with the shedding of her tears in anguished solitude. When she could not resist the pressure of her suffering any longer, and as she felt that she was in full possession of the treasured secrets of her heart, she took the quill and commenced mingling her tears with ink upon parchment, and she inscribed:

"My Beloved Sister,

"When the heart becomes congested with secrets, and the eyes begin to burn from the searing tears, and the ribs are about to burst with the growing of the heart's confinement, one cannot find expression for such a labyrinth except by a surge of release.

"Sorrowful persons find joy in lamentation, and lovers

encounter comfort and condolence in dreams, and the oppressed delight in receiving sympathy. I am writing to you now because I feel like a poet who fancies the beauty of objects whose impression he composes in verse while being ruled by a divine power.... I am like a child of the starving poor who cries for food, instigated by bitterness of hunger, disregarding the plight of his poor and merciful mother and her defeat in life.

"Listen to my painful story, my dear sister, and weep with me, for sobbing is like a prayer, and the tears of mercy are like a charity because they come forth from a living and sensitive and good soul and they are not shed in vain. It was the will of my father when I married a noble and rich man. My father was like most of the rich, whose only joy in life is to improve their wealth by adding more gold to their coffers in fear of poverty, and curry nobility with grandeur in anticipation of the attacks of the black days.... I find myself now, with all my love and dreams, a victim upon a golden altar which I hate, and an inherited honour which I despise.

"I respect my husband because he is generous and kind to all; he endeavours to bring happiness to me, and spends his gold to please my heart, but I have found that the impression of all these things is not worth one moment of a true and divine love. Do not ridicule me, my sister, for I am now a most enlightened person regarding the needs of a woman's heart—that throbbing heart which is like a bird flying in the spacious sky of love.... It is like a vase replenished with the wine of the ages that has been pressed for the sipping souls.... It is like a book in whose pages one reads the chapters of happiness and misery, joy and pain, laughter and sorrow. No one can read this book except the true companion who is the other half of the woman, created for her since the beginning of the world.

"Yes, I became most knowing amongst all women as to the purpose of the soul and meaning of the heart, for I have found that my magnificent horses and beautiful carriages and glittering coffers of gold and sublime nobility are not worth one glance from the eyes of that poor young man who is patiently waiting and suffering the pangs of bitterness and misery.... That youth who is oppressed by the cruelty and will of my father, and imprisoned in the narrow and melancholy jail of Life....

"Please, my dear, do not contrive to console me, for the calamity through which I have realized the power of my love is my great consoler. Now I am looking forward from behind my tears and awaiting the coming of Death to lead me to where I will meet the companion of my soul and embrace him as I did before we entered this strange world.

"Do not think evil of me, for I am doing my duty as a faithful wife, and complying calmly and patiently with the laws and rules of man. I honour my husband with my sense, and respect him with my heart, and revere him with my soul, but there is a withholding, for God gave part of me to my beloved before I knew him.

"Heaven willed that I spend my life with a man not meant for me, and I am wasting my days silently according to the will of Heaven; but if the gates of Eternity do not open, I will remain with the beautiful half of my soul and look back to the Past, and that Past is this Present.... I shall look at life as Spring looks at Winter, and contemplate the obstacles of Life as one who has climbed the rough trail and reached the mountain top."

❧

At that moment the maiden ceased writing and hid her face with her cupped hands and wept bitterly. Her heart declined to entrust to the pen its most sacred secrets, but resorted to the pouring of dry tears that dispersed quickly and mingled with the gentle ether, the haven of the lovers' souls and the flowers' spirits. After a moment she took the quill and added, "Do you remember that youth? Do you recollect the rays which emanated from his eyes, and the sorrowful signs upon his face? Do you recall that laughter which bespoke the tears of a mother, torn from her only child? Can you retrace his serene voice speaking the echo of a distant valley? Do you remember him meditating and staring longingly and calmly at objects and speaking of them in strange words, and then bending his head and sighing as if fearing to reveal the secrets of his great heart? Do you recall his dreams and beliefs? Do you recollect all these things in a youth whom humanity counts as one of her children and upon whom my father looked with eyes of superiority because he is higher than earthly greed and nobler than inherited grandeur?

"You know, my dear sister, that I am a martyr in this belittling world, and a victim of ignorance. Will you sympathize with a sister who sits in the silence of the horrible night pouring down the contents of her inner self and revealing to you her heart's secrets? I am sure that you will sympathize with me, for I know that Love has visited your heart."

❧

Dawn came, and the maiden surrendered herself to Slumber, hoping to find sweeter and more gentle dreams than those she had encountered in her awakeness....

2

The Ambitious Violet

There was a beautiful and fragrant violet who lived placidly amongst her friends, and swayed happily amidst the other flowers in a solitary garden. One morning, as her crown was embellished with beads of dew, she lifted her head and looked about; she saw a tall and handsome rose standing proudly and reaching high into space, like a burning torch upon an emerald lamp.

The violet opened her blue lips and said, "What an unfortunate am I among these flowers, and how humble is the position I occupy in their presence! Nature has fashioned me to be short and poor. . . . I live very close to the earth and I cannot raise my head toward the blue sky, or turn my face to the sun, as the roses do."

And the rose heard her neighbour's words; she laughed and commented, "How strange is your talk! You are fortunate, and yet you cannot understand your fortune. Nature has bestowed upon you fragrance and beauty which she did not grant to any other. . . . Cast aside your thoughts and be contented, and remember that he who humbles himself will be exalted, and he who exalts himself will be crushed."

The violet answered, "You are consoling me because you have that which I crave. . . . You seek to embitter me with the meaning that you are great.... How painful is the preaching of the fortunate to the heart of the miserable! And how severe is the strong when he stands as advisor among the weak!"

❧

And Nature heard the conversation of the violet and the rose; she approached and said, "What has happened to you, my daughter violet? You have been humble and sweet in all your deeds and words. Has greed entered your heart and numbed your senses?" In a pleading voice, the violet answered her, saying, "Oh great and merciful mother, full of love and sympathy, I beg you, with all my heart and soul, to grant my request and allow me to be a rose for one day."

And Nature responded, "You know not what you are seeking; you are unaware of the concealed disaster behind your blind ambition. If you were a rose you would be sorry, and repentance would avail you but naught." The violet insisted, "Change me into a tall rose, for I wish to lift my head high with pride; and regardless of my fate, it will be my own doing." Nature yielded, saying, "Oh ignorant and rebellious violet, I will grant your request. But if calamity befalls you, your complaint must be to yourself."

And Nature stretched forth her mysterious and magic fingers and touched the roots of the violet, who immediately turned into a tall rose, rising above all other flowers in the garden.

At eventide the sky became thick with black clouds, and the raging elements disturbed the silence of existence with thunder, and commenced to attack the garden, sending forth a great rain and strong winds. The tempest tore the branches and uprooted the plants and broke the stems of the tall flowers, sparing only the little ones who grew close to the friendly earth. That solitary garden suffered greatly from the belligerent skies, and when the storm calmed and the sky cleared, all the flowers were laid waste and none of them had escaped the wrath of Nature except the clan of small violets, hiding by the wall of the garden.

❧

Having lifted her head and viewed the tragedy of the flowers and trees, one of the violet maidens smiled happily and called to her companions, saying, "See what the tempest has done to the haughty flowers!" Another violet said, "We are small, and live close to the earth, but we are safe from the wrath of the skies." And a third one added, "Because we are poor in height the tempest is unable to subdue us."

At that moment the queen of violets saw by her side the converted violet, hurled to earth by the storm and distorted upon the wet grass like a limp soldier in a battle field. The queen of the violets lifted her head and called to her family, saying, "Look, my daughters, and meditate upon that which Greed has done to the violet who became a proud rose for one hour. Let the memory of this scene be a reminder of your good fortune."

And the dying rose moved and gathered the remnants of her strength, and quietly said, "You are contented and meek dullards; I have never feared the tempest. Yesterday I, too, was satisfied and contented with Life, but Contentment has acted as a barrier between my existence and the tempest of Life, confining me to a sickly and sluggish peace and tranquility of mind. I could have lived the same life you are living now by clinging with fear to the earth.... I could have waited for winter to shroud me with snow and deliver me to Death, who will surely claim all violets.... I am happy now because I have probed outside my little world into the mystery of the Universe...something which you have not yet done. I could have overlooked Greed, whose nature is higher than mine, but as I hearkened to the silence of the night, I heard the heavenly world talking to this earthly world, saying, 'Ambition beyond existence is the essential purpose of our being.' At that moment my spirit revolted and my heart longed for a position higher than my limited existence. I realized that the abyss cannot hear the song of the stars, and at that moment I commenced fighting against my smallness and craving for that which did not belong to me, until my rebelliousness turned into a great power, and my longing into a creating will....Nature, who is the great object of our deeper dreams, granted my request and changed me into a rose with her magic fingers."

The rose became silent for a moment, and in a weakening voice, mingled with pride and achievement, she said, "I have lived one hour as a proud rose; I have existed for a time like a queen; I have looked at the Universe from behind the eyes of the rose; I have heard the whisper of the firmament through the ears of the rose and touched the folds of Light's garment with rose petals. Is there any here who can claim such honour?" Having thus spoken, she lowered her head, and with a choking voice she gasped, "I shall die now, for my soul has attained its goal. I have finally extended my knowledge to a world beyond the narrow cavern of my birth. This is the design of Life....This is the secret of Existence." Then the rose quivered, slowly folded her petals, and breathed her last with a heavenly smile upon her lips...a smile of fulfillment of hope and purpose in Life...a smile of victory...a God's smile.

3

THE DAY OF MY BIRTH

It was on this day of the year that my
Mother brought me into the world; on
This day, a quarter-century past, the
Great silence placed me between the arms
Of Existence, replete with lamentation
And tears and conflicts.

Twenty five times have I encircled the
Blazing sun, and many times more has the
Moon encircled my smallness; yet, I have
Not learned the secrets of light, neither
Do I comprehend the mystery of darkness.

I have journeyed these twenty five years
With the earth and the sun and the planets
Through the Supreme Infinite; yet, my soul
Yearns for understanding of the Eternal Law
As the hollow grotto reverberates with the
Echo of the waves of the sea, but never fills.

Life exists through the existence of the
Heavenly system, but is not aware of the
Unbounded might of the firmament; and the
Soul sings the praise of the ebb and flow
Of a heavenly melody, but does not perceive
Its meaning.

Twenty five years past, the hand of Time
Recorded my being, and I am a living page
In the book of the universe; yet, I am now
But naught; but a vague word with meaning
Of complication symbolizing now nothing,
And then many things.

Meditations and memories, on this day of
Each year, congest my soul and halt the
Procession of life, revealing to me the
Phantoms of wasted nights, and sweeping
Them away as the great wind disperses the
Thin cloud from the horizon. And they
Vanish in the obscured corner of my hut
As the murmur of the narrow stream must
Vanish in the distant, broadened valley.

On this day of each year, the spirits
Which have fashioned my soul visit with
Me from all of Eternity and gather about
Me, chanting the sorrowful hymns of memories.
Then they retreat swiftly and disappear
Behind the visible objects like a flock of
Birds descending upon a deserted threshing

Floor whereupon they find no seeds; they
Hover in disappointment and depart quickly
For a more rewarding place.

On this day I meditate upon the past,
Whose purpose puzzles me in mind and
Confuses me in heart, and I look
Upon it as I look into a hazy mirror
In which I see naught but death-like
Countenances upon the past years.
As I gaze again, I see my own self
Staring upon my sorrowful self, and
I question Sorrow but find him mute.
Sorrow, if able to speak, would
Prove sweeter than the joy of song.

During my twenty five years of life
I have loved many things, and often
I loved that which the people hated,
And loathed that which the people
Loved.

And that which I loved when I was a
Child, I still love, and shall continue
To love forevermore. The power to
Love is God's greatest gift to man,
For it never will be taken from the
Blessed one who loves.

I love death, and entitle it with
Sweet names, and praise it with

Loving words, secretly and to the
Throngs of taunting listeners.

Although I have not renounced my great
Allegiance to death, I became deeply
Enamoured with life also, for life and
Death are equal to me in charm and
Sweetness and attraction, and they
Have joined hands in fostering in me
My longings and affections, and in
Sharing with me my love and suffering.

I love freedom, and my love for true
Freedom grew with my growing knowledge
Of the people's surrender to slavery
And oppression and tyranny, and of
Their submission to the horrible idols
Erected by the past ages and polished
By the parched lips of the slaves.

But I love those slaves with my love
For freedom, for they blindly kissed
The jaws of ferocious beasts in calm
And blissful unawareness, feeling not
The venom of the smiling vipers, and
Unknowingly digging their graves with
Their own fingers.

My love for freedom is my greatest love,
For I have found it to be a lovely
Maiden, frailed by aloneness and

Withered by solitude until she became
As a specter wandering in the midst
Of the dwellings unrecognized and
Unwelcome, and stopping by the waysides
And calling to the wayfarers who did
Not offer heed.

During this score and five years I have
Loved happiness as all men love happiness.
I was in constant search of her but did
Not find her in man's pathway; nor did
I observe the imprints of her footsteps
Upon the sand before man's palaces;
Neither did I hear the echo of her voice
From the windows of man's temples.

I sought happiness in my solitude, and
As I drew close to her I heard my soul
Whisper into my heart, saying, "The
Happiness you seek is a virgin, born
And reared in the depths of each heart,
And she emerges not from her birthplace."
And when I opened my heart to find her,
I discovered in its domain only her
Mirror and her cradle and her raiment,
And happiness was not there.

I love mankind and I love equally all
Three human kinds...the one who
Blasphemes life, the one who blesses
It, and the one who meditates upon it.

I love the first for his misery and
The second for his generosity and the
Third for his perception and peace.

❧

Thus, with love, did five and twenty
Years race into nothingness, and thus
Swiftly sped the days and the nights,
Falling from the roadway of my life
And fluttering away like the drying
Leaves of the trees before the winds of
Autumn.

Today I stopped on my road, like the
Weary traveler who has not reached his
Destination but seeks to ascertain his
Position. I look in every direction, but
Cannot find trace of any part of my past
At which I might point and say, "This is
Mine!"

Nor can I reap harvest from the seasons
Of my years, for my bins boast only
These parchments upon which the black
Ink is traced, and these paintings,
Upon which appear simple lines and colours.

With these papers and pictures I have
Succeeded only in shrouding and burying
My love and my thoughts and my dreams,
Even as the sower buries the seeds in

The heart of the earth.

But when the sower sows the seeds in
The heart of the earth he returns home
At eventide, hoping and waiting for
The day of harvest; but I have sown
The inner seeds of my heart in despair,
And hoping and waiting are in vain.

And now, since I have made my five and
Twenty journeys about the sun, I look
Upon the past from behind a deep veil
Of sighs and sorrows, and the silent
Future enlightens itself to me only
Through the sad lamp of the past.

I stare at the universe through the
Transom of my hut and behold the faces
Of men, and hear their voices rise into
Space and hear their footsteps falling
Into the stones; and I perceive the
Revelations of their spirits and the
Vibrations of their desires and the
Throbbing of their hearts.

And I see the children, running and
Laughing and playing and crying; and
I observe the youths walking with their
Heads lifted upward as if reading and
Singing the Kaseeda of youth between
The margins of their eyes, lined with

The radiant rays of the sun.

And I behold the maidens, who are walking
Gracefully and swaying like tender
Branches, and smiling like flowers, and
Gazing upon the youths from behind the
Quivering eyes of love.

And I see the aged walking slowly with
Bent backs, leaning upon their walking
Staffs, staring at the earth as though
Seeking there a treasure lost in youth.

I observe these images and phantoms
Moving and crawling in the paths and
Roadways of the city.

Then I look beyond the city and meditate
Upon the wilderness and its revered
Beauty and its speaking silence; its
Knolls and valleys and lofty trees; its
Fragrant flowers and brisk brooks and
Singing birds.

Then I look beyond the wilderness and
Contemplate the sea with all the magical
Wonders and secrets of its depths, and
The foaming and raging waves of its
Surface. The depths are calm.

Then I gaze beyond the ocean and see the

Infinite sky with its glittering stars;
And its suns and moons and planets; its
Gigantic forces and its myriad elements
That comply unerringly with a great
Law possessing neither a beginning nor
An ending.

Upon these things I ponder from between
My walls, forgetting my twenty five
Years and all the years which preceded
Them and all the centuries to come.

❧

At this moment my own existence and
All of my environs seem as the weak
Sigh of a small child trembling in the
Deep and eternal emptiness of a supreme
And boundless space.

But this insignificant entity...
This self which is myself, and whose
Motion and clamour I hear constantly,
Is now lifting strengthening wings
Toward the spacious firmament,
Extending hands in all directions,
Swaying and shivering upon this day
Which brought me into life, and life
Into me.

And then a tremendous voice arises
From the Holy of Holies within me,

Saying, "Peace be with you, Life!
Peace be with you, Awakening!
Peace be with you, Revelation!
Peace be with you, oh Day, who
Engulfs the darkness of the earth
With thy brilliant light!
"Peace be with you, oh Night,
Through whose darkness the lights
Of heaven sparkle!
"Peace be with you, Seasons of the
Year!
Peace be with you, Spring, who
Restores the earth to youth!
Peace be with you, Summer, who
Heralds the glory of the sun!
Peace be with you, Autumn, who
Gives with joy the fruits of
Labour and the harvest of toil!
Peace be with you, Winter, whose
Rage and tempest restore to
Nature her sleeping strength!
"Peace be with you, Years, who
Reveal what the years concealed!
Peace be with you, Ages, who
Build what the ages destroyed!
Peace be with you, Time, who leads
Us to the fullness of death!
Peace be with you, Heart, who
Throbs in peace while submerged

In tears!
Peace be with you, Lips, who
Utter joyous words of salaam while
Tasting the gall and the vinegar
Of life!
Peace be with you, Soul, who
Directs the rudder of life and
Death while hidden from us
Behind the curtain of the sun!"

4

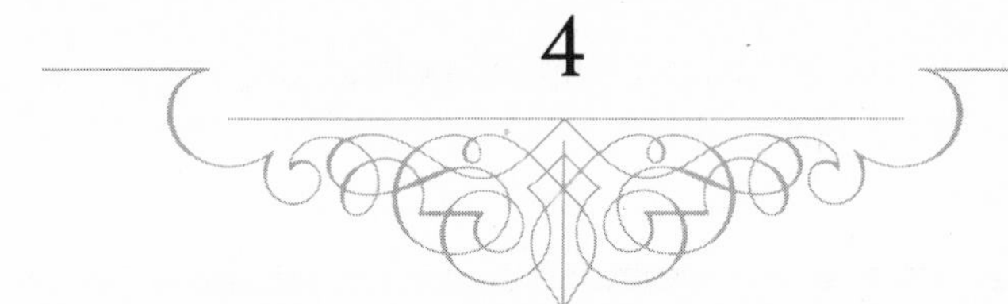

Sayings

I discovered the secret of the sea in meditation upon the dewdrop.

❧

Where can I find a man governed by reason instead of habits and urges?

❧

As one's gifts increase, his friends decrease.

❧

If you are poor, shun association with him who measures men with the yardstick of riches.

❧

I prefer to be a dreamer among the humblest, with visions to be realized, than lord among those without dreams and desires.

❧

Of life's two chief prizes, beauty and truth, I found the first in a loving heart and the second in a laborer's hand.

❧

People speak of plague with fear and tremor, yet of

destroyers like Alexander and Napoleon they speak with ecstatic reverence.

❧

Thrift is being generous, to all except the misers.

❧

I saw them eating and I knew who they were.

❧

No lower can a man descend than to interpret his dreams into gold and silver.

❧

Someone said to a stubborn prattler, "Your conversation soothes and cures the ailing heart." Whereat he hushed and claimed to be a medical doctor.

❧

What shall I say of the man who slaps me when I kiss him on the face and who kisses my foot when I slap him?

❧

How hard is the life of him who asks for love and receives passion!

❧

To be closer to God, be closer to people.

❧

Marriage is either death or life; there is no betwixt and between.

❧

Keep me from the man who says, "I am a candle to light people on their way"; but to the one who seeks to make his way through the light of the people, bring me nearer.

❧

It is slavery to live in the mind unless it has become part of the body.

❦

Some silky faces are lined with coarse cloth.

❦

Some think I wink at them when I shut my eyes to avoid their sight.

❦

My proof convinces the ignorant, and the wise man's proof convinces me. But he whose reasoning falls between wisdom and ignorance, I neither can convince him, nor can he convince me.

❦

If reward is the goal of religion, if patriotism serves self-interest, and if education is pursued for advancement, then I would prefer to be a non-believer, a non-patriot, and a humbly ignorant man.

❦

An epoch will come when people will disclaim kinship with us as we disclaim kinship with the monkeys.

❦

Some hear with their ears, some with their stomachs, some with their pockets; and some hear not at all.

❦

Some souls are like sponges. You cannot squeeze anything out of them except what they have sucked from you.

❦

If there were two men alike, the world would not be big enough to contain them.

This is the history of man: birth, marriage, and death; and birth, marriage, and death; and birth, marriage, and death. But then a madman with strange ideas appears before the people and tells a dream of a different world whose more cultured beings see more in their dreams than birth, marriage, and death.

He brings disaster upon his nation who never sows a seed, or lays a brick, or weaves a garment, but makes politics his occupation.

By adornment one acknowledges his ugliness.

They say that silence resides in contentment; but I say to you that denial, rebellion, and contempt dwell in silence.

I have yet to meet an ignorant man whose roots are not embedded in my soul.

Truth is the daughter of Inspiration; analysis and debate keep the people away from Truth.

He who forgives you for a sin you have not committed forgives himself for his own crime.

The foundling is an infant whose mother conceived him between love and faith, and gave birth to him between the fear and frenzy of death. She swaddled him with a living remnant of her heart and placed him at the orphanage gate and departed with her head bent under the heavy burden of her cross. And to complete her tragedy, you and I taunted her: "What a disgrace, what a disgrace!"

Ambition is a sort of work.

The partition between the sage and the fool is more slender than the spider web.

Some seek pleasure in pain; and some cannot cleanse themselves except with filth.

The fear of hell is hell itself, and the longing for paradise is paradise itself.

We must not forget that there are still cave dwellers; the caves are our hearts.

We may change with the seasons, but the seasons will not change us.

Three things I like in literature: rebellion, perfection, and the abstract. And the three things I hate in it are imitation, distortion, and complexity.

If you choose between two evils, let your choice fall on the obvious rather than the hidden, even though the first appears greater than the second.

Deliver me from him who does not tell the truth unless

he stings; and from the man of good conduct and bad intentions; and from him who acquires self-esteem by finding fault in others.

Does the song of the sea end at the shore or in the hearts of those who listen to it?

The rich claim kinship with those of noble birth; and the nobly-born seek marriages among the rich; and each despises the other.

Most of us hover dubiously between mute rebellion and prattling submission.

The ill-intentioned always fall short of achieving their purpose.

The supreme state of the soul is to obey even that against which the mind rebels. And the lowest state of the mind is to revolt against that which the soul obeys.

They feed me the milk of their sympathy; if only they knew that I was weaned of such pap from the day of my birth.

The spiritual man is he who has experienced all earthly things and is in revolt against them.

Strange that virtue in me brings me nothing but harm, while my evil has never been to my disadvantage.

Nevertheless, I continue fanatic in my virtue.

❧

Oh, heart, if the ignorant say to you that the soul perishes like the body, answer that the flower perishes, but the seeds remain. This is the law of God.

❧

If you wish to see the valleys, climb to the mountain top; if you desire to see the mountain top, rise into the cloud; but if you seek to understand the cloud, close your eyes and think.

❧

Life kisses us on both cheeks
Day and morn,
But laughs at our deeds
Eve and dawn.

❧

Listen to the woman when she looks at you, but not when she talks to you.

❧

Affection is the youth of the heart, and thought is the heart's maturity; but oratory is its senility.

❧

Which one of us listens to the hymn of the brook when the tempest speaks.

❧

Hard is life for him who desires death but lives on for the sake of his beloved ones.

❧

I was wandering in unexplored places of the earth when I was seized and made a slave. Then I was freed and became an ordinary citizen, and, in turn, a merchant, a scholar, a minister, a king, a tyrant. After being dethroned I became a rioter, a hoodlum, an impostor, a vagrant, then a slave lost in the unexplored realm of my soul.

❧

As between the soul and the body there is a bond, so are the body and its environment linked together.

❧

Be not contented with little; he who brings to the springs of life an empty jar will return with two full ones.

❧

He who looks upon us through the eyes of God will see our naked and essential reality.

❧

God made Truth with many doors to welcome every believer who knocks on them.

❧

The flower that grows above the clouds will never wither. And the song chanted by the lips of the brides of dawn will never vanish.

❧

He who philosophizes is like a mirror that reflects objects that it cannot see, like a cave that returns the echo of voices that it does not hear.

❧

The poet is he who makes you feel, after reading his poem, that his best verses have not yet been composed.

❧

The tyrant calls for sweet wine from sour grapes.

❧

Who among men can stroll on the bottom of the sea as if promenading in a garden?

❧

Do you believe you can comprehend the substances by inquiring about the purposes? Can you tell the flavor of the wine by looking at the wine jug?

❧

From my obscurity came forth a light and illuminated my path.

❧

Our souls traverse spaces in Life which are not measurable by Time, that invention of man.

❧

He who reveals to himself what his conscience has prohibited commits a sin. And he also is a sinner who denies himself what his conscience has revealed.

❧

Poetry is the secret of the soul; why babble it away in words?

❧

Poetry is the understanding of the whole. How can you communicate it to him who understands but the part?

❧

Poetry is a flame in the heart, but rhetoric is flakes of snow. How can flame and snow be joined together?

❧

How gravely the glutton counsels the famished to bear the pangs of hunger.

❧

Representative governments were, in the past, the

fruits of revolutions; today they are economic consequences.

A feeble nation weakens its strong ones and strengthens the weak ones of a powerful nation.

The heartbreak of love sings, the sadness of knowledge speaks, the melancholy of desire whispers, and the anguish of poverty weeps. But there is a sorrow deeper than love, loftier than knowledge, stronger than desire, and more bitter than poverty. It is mute and has no voice; its eyes glitter like stars.

The secret in singing is found between the vibration in the singer's voice and the throb in the hearer's heart.

Love is a trembling happiness.

A singer cannot delight you with his singing unless he himself delights to sing.

When, in misfortune, you seek commiseration from your neighbor, you give him a part of your heart. If he is good-hearted, he will thank you; if he is hard-hearted, he will scorn you.

You progress not through improving what has been done, but reaching toward what has yet to be done.

A sage met with a stupid magnate and they discussed

education and wealth. When they separated, the sage found naught in his hand save a handful of dirt, and the magnate discovered nothing in his heart but a puff of mist.

❧

The truth that needs proof is only half true.

❧

Keep me from the wisdom that does not weep, and the philosophy that does not laugh, and the pride that does not bow its head before a child.

❧

Among the people there are killers who have not yet shed blood, and thieves who have stolen nothing, and liars who have so far told the truth.

❧

At ebb tide I wrote
A line upon the sand
And gave it all my heart
And all my soul.
At flood tide I returned
To read what I had inscribed
And found my ignorance upon the shore.

❧

He is short-sighted who looks only on the path he treads and the wall on which he leans.

❧

They think virtue is that which harasses me and relieves my neighbor, and sin that which relieves me and harasses my neighbor. Let them know that I can be either saint or sinner away from them in my hermitage.

❧

Examine your yesterday's ledger and you will find that

you are still indebted to people and to life.

❦

Tenderness and kindness are not signs of weakness and despair, but manifestations of strength and resolution.

❦

Poverty may veil arrogance, and the pain of calamity may seek the mask of pretense.

❦

The hungry savage picks a fruit from the tree and eats it. The hungry citizen in civilized society buys a fruit from the one who bought it from another who bought it from him who picked it from the tree.

❦

When I planted my pain in the field of patience it bore fruit of happiness.

❦

Art is a step in the known toward the unknown.

❦

The Nine Woes

Woe to the nation that departs from religion to belief, from country lane to city alley, from wisdom to logic.

Woe to the nation that does not weave what it wears, nor plant what it eats, nor press the wine that it drinks.

Woe to the conquered nation that sees the victor's pomp as the perfection of virtue, and in whose eyes the ugliness of the conqueror is beauty.

Woe to the nation that combats injury in its dream but yields to the wrong in its wakefulness.

Woe to the nation that does not raise its voice save in a funeral, that shows esteem only at the grave, that waits to rebel until its neck is under the edge of the sword.

Woe to the nation whose politics is subtlety, whose philosophy is jugglery, whose industry is patching.

Woe to the nation that greets a conqueror with fife and drum, then hisses him off to greet another conqueror with trumpet and song.

Woe to the nation whose sage is voiceless, whose champion is blind, whose advocate is a prattler.

Woe to the nation in which each tribe claims to be a nation.

❧

Education sows not seeds in you, but makes your seeds grow.

❧

You eat in a hurry but are leisurely when you walk. Why, then, don't you eat with your feet and walk on the palms of your hand?

❧

On the scholar who was made of thought and affection, speech was bestowed. On the researcher who was made of speech, a little thought and affection were bestowed.

❧

Enthusiasm is a volcano on whose top never grows the grass of hesitation.

❧

The millstone may break down but the river continues its course to the sea.

❧

Inspiration is in seeing a part of the whole with the part of the whole in you.

❧

Contradiction is the lowest form of intelligence.

❧

The believer is led to doubt justice when he sees the trick of the fox triumph over the justice of the lion.

❧

Fear of the devil is one way of doubting God.

❧

Slaves are the faults of the kings.

❧

The difficulty we meet with in reaching our goal is the shortest path to it.

❧

They tell me, "If you find a slave asleep, don't wake him up; he may be dreaming of freedom." And I reply, "If you find a slave asleep, wake him and talk to him about freedom."

❧

In the magnifying glass of man's eye the world looks greater than it is.

❧

When the earth exhales it gives birth to us. When it inhales death is our lot.

❧

That which we call intelligence in the mind of some people is but a local inflammation.

❧

Art arises when the secret vision of the artist and the manifestation of nature agree to find new shapes.

❦

Martyrdom is the voluntary falling of the supreme soul to the level of the fallen one.

❦

Compulsion is a mirror in which he who looks for long will see his inner self endeavoring to commit suicide.

❦

That which you think is ugly is but the treachery of the outer directed at the inner self.

❦

We are all practical in our own interest and idealists when it concerns others.

❦

I pity him whose lips and tongue writhe with words of praise while his hand is outstretched in beggary.

❦

He is virtuous who does not acquit himself of the people's faults.

❦

To realize that prophecy in the people is like fruit in the tree is to know the unity of life.

❦

History does not repeat itself except in the minds of those who do not know history.

❦

Evil is an unfit creature, laggard in obeying the law of the continuity of fitness.

Why do some people scoop from your sea and boast of their rivulet?

He is free who carries the slave's burden with patience.

Beauty in the heart that longs for it is more sublime than in the eyes of him who sees it.

Every innovator is a reformer. If he is right, he leads the people to the right path. If he is wrong, the fanaticism he rouses in them heartens them to stand for their right.

Sayings remain meaningless until they are embodied in habits.

The necessity for explanation is a sign of weakness in the text.

Faith is a knowledge within the heart, beyond the reach of proof.

Humanity is divinity divided without and united within.

He who comes clothed in his best at his neighbor's funeral will wear rags at his son's wedding.

According to the Arabic proverb, there are no such

things as a Phoenix, a Ghoul, or a True Bosom Friend; but I say to you that I found them all among my neighbors.

❦

The creator gives no heed to the critic unless he becomes a barren inventor.

❦

Prosperity comes through two things: exploitation of the earth and distribution of its produce.

❦

The just is close to the people's hearts, but the merciful is close to the heart of God.

❦

Irregularity comes either from madness or from ingenuity.

❦

He who pities woman depreciates her. He who attributes to her the evils of society oppresses her. He who thinks her goodness is of his goodness and her evil of his evil is shameless in his pretensions. But he who accepts her as God made her does her justice.

❦

Poverty is a temporary fault, but excessive wealth is a lasting ailment.

❦

Remembrance is a tripping stone in the path of Hope.

❦

Our worst fault is our preoccupation with the faults of others.

❦

I never speak without error, for my thoughts come

from the world of abstraction and my statements from the world of reference.

Poetry is a flash of lightning; it becomes mere composition when it is an arrangement of words.

Had it not been for seeing and hearing, light and sound would have been naught but confusion and pulsations in space. Likewise, had it not been for the heart you love, you would have been a fine dust blown and scattered by the wind.

Passionate love is a quenchless thirst.

No one believes the sincere except the honest.

If you wish to understand a woman, watch her mouth when she smiles; but to study a man, observe the whiteness of his eyes when he is angry.

The Arts of the Nations

The art of the Egyptians is in the occult.
The art of the Chaldeans is in calculation.
The art of the Greeks is in proportion.
The art of the Romans is in echo.
The art of the Chinese is in etiquette.
The art of the Hindus is in the weighing of good and evil.
The art of the Jews is in the sense of doom.

The art of the Arabs is in reminiscence and exaggeration.

The art of the Persians is in fastidiousness.

The art of the French is in finesse.

The art of the English is in analysis and self-righteousness.

The art of the Spaniards is in fanaticism.

The art of the Italians is in beauty.

The art of the Germans is in ambition.

The art of the Russians is in sadness.

❧

Someone gave me a lamb and I gave him a she-camel. Then he offered me two lambs and I repaid him with two she-camels. Later he came to my sheepfold and counted my nine camels. Then he gave me nine lambs.

❧

The most useful among the people is he who is distant from the people.

❧

Your self consists of two selves; one imagines that he knows himself and the other that the people know him.

❧

Science and religion are in full accord, but science and faith are in complete discord.

❧

Subjects are the most anxious to learn about kings.

❧

Nursing a patient is a sort of embalming.

❧

If existence had not been better than non-existence,

there would have been no being.

❦

When you attain your pilgrimage, you will see everything beautiful even in eyes that never saw beauty.

❦

I shall cast my jewels to the pigs so that they may swallow them and die either of gluttony or indigestion.

❦

Can one sing whose mouth is full of filth?

❦

When affection withers, it intellectualizes.

❦

Poets are two kinds: an intellectual with an acquired personality, and an inspired one who was a self before his human training began. But the difference between intelligence and inspiration in poetry is like the difference between sharp fingernails that mangle the skin and ethereal lips that kiss and heal the body's sores.

❦

To understand the heart and mind of a person, look not at what he has already achieved, but at what he aspires to do.

❦

He who stares at the small and near images will have difficulty in seeing and distinguishing those that are great and remote.

❦

I am abashed by eulogies, but the eulogist rants on and makes me appear shameless before the whole world.

❦

When I meditated upon Jesus I always saw him either as an infant in the manger seeing His mother Mary's face for the first time, or, staring from the crucifix at His mother Mary's face for the last time.

❦

We are all warriors in the battle of Life, but some lead and others follow.

❦

Souls are fires whose ashes are the bodies.

❦

The pen is a sceptre, but how scarce kings are among the writers!

❦

He who conceals his intention behind flowery words of praise is like a woman who seeks to hide her ugliness behind cosmetics.

❦

If I knew the cause of my ignorance, I would be a sage.

❦

The butterfly will continue to hover over the field and the dewdrops will still glitter upon the grass when the pyramids of Egypt are levelled and the skyscrapers of New York are no more.

❦

How can we hear the song of the field while our ears have the clamor of the city to swallow?

❦

Trading is thieving unless it is barter.

❦

The best of men is he who blushes when you praise

him and remains silent when you defame him.

The pain that accompanies love, invention, and responsibility also gives delight.

What a man reveals differs from what he conceals as rain that falls over the fields differs from the cloud that looms over the mountains.

The chemist who can extract from his heart's elements compassion, respect, longing, patience, regret, surprise, and forgiveness and compound them into one can create that atom which is called LOVE.

He who requires urging to do a noble act will never accomplish it.

The strong grows in solitude where the weak withers away.

They say if one understands himself, he understands all people. But I say to you, when one loves people, he learns something about himself.

No one has prevented me from doing something who is not himself interested in it.

Fame burdens the shoulders of an excellent man, and by the way he carries the load people judge him. If he carries his burden unhaltingly he will be promoted to the rank of hero; but if his foot slips and he falls, he is counted among the impostors.

❧

The optimist sees the rose and not its thorns; the pessimist stares at the thorns, oblivious of the rose.

❧

Wishes and desires are Life's occupation. We must strive to realize Life's wishes and execute its desires whether we will or no.

❧

He who fails to understand Socrates' character is spellbound by Alexander; when he cannot comprehend Virgil, he praises Caesar; if his mind cannot discern Laplace's thought, he blows his horn and beats his drum for Napoleon. And I have taken note that in the minds of those who admire Alexander, Caesar, or Napoleon I always found a touch of servitude.

❧

When man invents a machine, he runs it; then the machines begin to run him, and he becomes the slave of his slave.

❧

The virtue of some of the rich is that they teach us to despise wealth.

❧

Oratory is the cunning of the tongue over the ear, but eloquence is the joining of the heart with the soul.

❧

Civilization commenced when man first dug the earth and sowed seeds.

Religion began when man discerned the sun's compassion on the seeds which he sowed in the earth.

Art began when man glorified the sun with a hymn of gratitude.

Philosophy began when man ate the produce of the earth and suffered indigestion.

Man's value is in the few things he creates and not in the many possessions he amasses.

There is no true wealth beyond a man's need.

Every nation is responsible for each act of its individuals.

Who can separate himself from his sorrows and solitude without suffering in his heart?

Because voice need not carry the tongue and the lips on its wings, it penetrates the sky; so, too, the eagle need not carry its nest, but soars alone in the spacious firmament.

Love knows not its depth till the hour of separation.

Faith perceives Truth sooner than Experience can.

Most writers mend their tattered thoughts with patches from dictionaries.

Inhibitions and religious prohibitions do more harm than anarchy.

The nets of the law are devised to catch small criminals only.

Feigned modesty is imprudence adorned.

Courage, which is the sixth sense, finds the shortest way to triumph.

Chastity of the body may be miserliness of the spirit.

Keep me safe, Lord, from the tongue of the viper, and of him who fails to obtain the fame he craves.

I never met a conceited man whom I did not find inwardly embarrassed.

We fear death, yet we long for slumber and beautiful dreams.

Some who are too scrupulous to steal your possessions nevertheless see no wrong in tampering with your thoughts.

Our sorrow over the dead may be a sort of jealousy.

❦

We all admire strength, but the majority is most impressed by it when it is without form and stability. Few are those who respect strength when it is clearly defined and has meaningful ends.

❦

The light of stars that were extinguished ages ago still reaches us. So is it with great men who died centuries ago, but still reach us with the radiations of their personality.

❦

The sultan of sultans is he who has gained the love of the pauper.

❦

There is no convenience in our present-day civilization that does not cause discomfort.

❦

Your confidence in the people, and your doubt about them, are closely related to your self-confidence and your self-doubt.

❦

We demand freedom of speech and freedom of press, although we have nothing to say and nothing worth printing.

❦

To you who praise the "happy medium" to me as the way of life, I reply, "Who wants to be lukewarm between cold and hot, or tremble between life and death, or be a jelly, neither fluid nor solid?"

❦

Strength and tolerance are partners.

❦

Love and emptiness in us are like the sea's ebb and flow.

❦

Poverty hides itself in thought before it surrenders to purses.

❦

Man merely discovers; he never can and never will invent.

❦

Philosophy's work is finding the shortest path between two points.

❦

Would it not be more economical for the governments to build asylums for the sane instead of the demented?

❦

The most solid stone in the structure is the lowest one in the foundation.

❦

When I wrote on my door:
"Leave your traditions outside,
Before you come in,"
Not a soul dared
To visit me or open my door.

❦

Even the laws of Life obey Life's laws.

❦

I learned to be daring from the indolence of my people.

❦

He is most worthy of praise from whom the people unjustly withhold it.

The truly religious man does not embrace a religion; and he who embraces one has no religion.

Most men with delicate feelings hasten to hurt your feelings lest you precede them and hurt theirs.

The writer who draws his material from a book is like one who borrows money only to lend it.

When I didn't reward
One who eulogized me,
He grumbled and complained.
I suffered it in silence
And the people laughed at him.

Distinguish between the gift that is an insult and the gift that is a token of respect.

The one who disagrees is more talked about than the one who agrees.

I never doubted a truth that needed an explanation unless I found myself having to analyze the explanation.

Sweetness is closer to bitterness than it is to decay, no matter how sweetish its smell.

The essence of everything on earth, seen and unseen,

is spiritual. On entering the invisible city my body is covered by my spirit. Who so seeks to cleave the body from the spirit, or the spirit from the body is turning his heart away from the truth. The flower and its fragrance are one; they are blind who deny the color and the image of the flower, saying that it possesses only a fragrance vibrating in the ether. They are like those, deficient in the sense of smell, to whom flowers are nought but shapes and hues without fragrance.

Everything in creation exists within you, and everything in you exists in creation. You are in borderless touch with the closest things, and, what is more, distance is not sufficient to separate you from things far away. All things from the lowest to the loftiest, from the smallest to the greatest, exist within you as equal things. In one atom are found all the elements of the earth. One drop of water contains all the secrets of the oceans. In one motion of the mind are found all the motions of all the laws of existence.

❧

God has placed in each soul an apostle to lead us upon the illumined path. Yet many seek life from without, unaware that it is within them.

❧

In education the life of the mind proceeds gradually from scientific experiments to intellectual theories, to spiritual feeling, and then to God.

❧

We are still busy examining sea shells as if they were all that emerge from the sea of life to the shore of day and night.

❧

The tree that contrives to cheat life by living in the

shade; withers when it is removed and replanted in the sun.

❦

Languages, governments, and religions are formed from the golden dust that rises from both sides of the road on which man's magnificent life proceeds.

❦

The Spirit of the West is our friend if we accept him, but our enemy if we are possessed by him; our friend if we open our hearts to him, our enemy if we yield him our hearts; our friend if we take from that which suits us, our enemy if we let ourselves be used to suit him.

❦

Exhaustion dooms every nation and every people; it is drowsy agony, death in a sort of slumber.

❦

The potter can fashion a wine jug from clay, but nothing out of sand and gravel.

❦

Wailing and lamentation befit those who stand before the throne of life and depart without leaving in its hands a drop of the sweat of their brows or the blood of their hearts.

❦

We devour the bread of charity because we are hungry; it revives, then slays us.

❦

How ugly is affection that lays a stone on one side of a structure and destroys a wall on the other side!

❦

How savage is love that plants a flower and uproots a field; that revives us for a day and stuns us for an age!

The means of reviving a language lie in the heart of the poet and upon his lips and between his fingers. The poet is the mediator between the creative power and the people. He is the wire that transmits the news of the world of spirit to the world of research. The poet is the father and mother of the language, which goes wherever he goes. When he dies, it remains prostrate over his grave, weeping and forlorn, until another poet comes to uplift it.

The calamity of the sons lies in the endowments of the parents. And he who does not deny them will remain the slave of Death until he dies.

The tremors of people shaken by the storm of life makes them appear alive. But in reality they have been dead since the day of their birth; and they lie unburied and the stench of decay rises from their bodies.

The dead tremble before the tempest, but the living walk with it.

Strange are the self-worshipers, since they worship carrion.

There are mysteries within the soul which no hypothesis can uncover and no guess can reveal.

Because he was born in fear and lives a coward, man hides in the crevices of the earth when he sees the tempest coming.

❧

The bird has an honor that man does not have. Man lives in the traps of his fabricated laws and traditions; but the birds live according to the natural law of God who causes the earth to turn around the sun.

❧

Believing is one thing, doing another. Many talk like the sea but their lives are stagnant marshes. Others raise their heads above the mountain tops, while their souls cling to the dark walls of caves.

❧

Worship does not require seclusion and solitude.

❧

Prayer is the song of the heart that makes its way to the throne of God even when entangled in the wailing of thousands of souls.

❧

God made our bodies temples for our souls, and they should be kept strong and clean to be worthy of the deity that occupies them.

❧

How distant I am from the people when I am with them, and how close when they are far away.

❧

People respect motherhood only when it wears the raiment of their laws.

❧

Love, like death, changes everything.

❧

The souls of some people are like school blackboards

on which Time writes signs, rules, and examples that are immediately erased with a wet sponge.

❧

The reality of music is in that vibration that remains in the ear after the singer finishes his song and the player no longer plucks the strings.

❧

What shall I say about him who borrows from me the money to buy a sword with which to attack me?

❧

My enemy said to me, "Love your enemy." And I obeyed him and loved myself.

❧

The black said to the white, "If you were grey I would be lenient with you."

❧

Many who know the price of everything are ignorant of its value.

❧

Every man's history is written upon his forehead, but in a language none but he who receives revelations can read.

❧

Show me your mother's face; I will tell you who you are.

❧

I know his father; how do you expect me not to know *him*?

❧

The freedom of the one who boasts of it is a slavery.

Some people do not publicly thank me in order to express their gratitude but to make public their perception of my talent in order to be admired themselves.

Good taste is not in making the right choice, but in perceiving in something the natural unity between its quantities and qualities.

The coarseness of some is preferable to the gentleness of others.

When people abhor what they cannot comprehend, they are like those burning with fever, to whom the choicest food is unpalatable.

I love the smooth-faced children; and also the bearded elders, if they have truly risen from the cradle and the swaddling band.

The wolf preys upon the lamb in the dark of the night, but the blood stains remain to accuse him by day.

Persecution does not make the just man to suffer, nor does oppression destroy him if he is on the right side of Truth. Socrates smiled as he took poison, and Stephen smiled as he was stoned. What truly hurts is our conscience that aches when we oppose it, and dies when we betray it.

The marching ages trample man's works; but they do

not obliterate his dreams, nor weaken his creative impulses. These remain because they are part of the Eternal Spirit, though they hide or sleep now and then, imitating the sun at nightfall and the moon at dawn.

❧

The young Lebanese woman is like a spring that gushes from the heart of the earth and flows through winding valleys. Since it cannot find an outlet to the sea, it turns into a calm lake that reflects upon its growing surface the glittering stars and the shining moon.

❧

Have I not survived hunger and thirst, suffering and mockery for the sake of the truth which heaven has awakened in my heart?

❧

Truth is the will and purpose of God in man.

❧

I shall follow the path to wherever my destiny and my mission for Truth shall take me.

❧

The man who inherits his wealth builds his mansion with money taken from the weak and the poor.

❧

The last steps of the slaughtered bird are painful, involuntary and unknowing; but those who witness that grisly dance know what caused it.

❧

He is a traitor who uses the Gospel as a threat to extract money...a hypocrite who uses the cross as a sword...a wolf disguised in a lamb's skin...a glutton who adores the tables more than the altars... a gold-hungry creature who runs after the rolling coin to the farthest land... a cheat who pilfers from widows and orphans. He is a monstrous being, with an eagle's beak, a tiger's claws, a hyena's teeth, and viper's fangs.

❧

God has placed a torch in your hearts that glows with knowledge and beauty; it is a sin to extinguish that torch and bury it in the ashes.

❧

God has created your spirits with wings to fly in the spacious firmament of Love and Freedom. How pitiful to lop off your wings with your own hands and suffer your spirit to crawl like vermin upon the earth.

5

Silent Sorrow

My neighbors, you remember the dawn of youth with pleasure and regret its passing; but I remember it like a prisoner who recalls the bars and shackles of his jail. You speak of those years between infancy and youth as a golden era free from confinement and cares, but I call those years an era of silent sorrow which dropped as a seed into my heart and grew with it and could find no outlet to the world of knowledge and wisdom until love came and opened the heart's doors and lighted its corners. Love provided me with a tongue and tears. You people remember the gardens and orchids and the meeting places and street corners that witnessed your games and heard your innocent whispering; and I remember, too, the beautiful spot in North Lebanon. Every time I close my eyes I see those valleys full of magic and dignity and those mountains covered with glory and greatness trying to reach the sky. Every time I shut my ears to the clamor of the city I hear the murmur of the rivulets and the rustling of the branches. All those beauties which I speak of now and which I long to see, as a child longs for his mother's breast, wounded my spirit, imprisoned in the darkness of youth, as a falcon suffers in its cage when it sees a flock of birds flying freely in the spacious sky. Those valleys and hills fired my imagination, but bitter thoughts wove round my heart a net of hopelessness.

Every time I went to the fields I returned disappointed, without understanding the cause of my disappointment. Every time I looked at the gray sky I felt my heart contract. Every time I heard the singing of the birds and babbling of the spring I suffered without understanding the reason for my suffering. It is said that unsophistication makes a man empty and that emptiness makes him carefree. It may be true among those who were born dead and who exist like frozen corpses; but the sensitive boy who feels much and knows little is the most unfortunate creature under the sun, because he is torn by two forces. The first force elevates him and shows him the beauty of existence through a cloud of dreams; the second ties him down to the earth and fills his eyes with dust and overpowers him with fears and darkness.

Solitude has soft, silky hands, but with strong fingers it grasps the heart and makes it ache with sorrow. Solitude is the ally of sorrow as well as a companion of spiritual exaltation.

The boy's soul undergoing the buffeting of sorrow is like a white lily just unfolding. It trembles before the breeze and opens its heart to daybreak and folds its leaves back when the shadow of night comes. If that boy does not have diversion or friends or companions in his games, his life will be like a narrow prison in which he sees nothing but spiderwebs and hears nothing but the crawling of insects.

That sorrow which obsessed me during my youth was not caused by lack of amusement, because I could have had it; neither from lack of friends, because I could have found them. That sorrow was caused by an inward ailment which made me love solitude. It killed in me the inclination for games and amusement. It removed from my shoulders the wings of youth and made me like a pond of water between mountains which reflects in its calm surface the shadows of ghosts and the colors of clouds and trees, but cannot find an outlet by which to pass singing to the sea.

Thus was my life before I attained the age of eighteen. That year is like a mountain peak in my life, for it awakened knowledge in me and made me understand the vicissitudes of mankind. In that year I was reborn and unless a person is born again his life will remain like a blank sheet in the book of existence. In that year, I saw the angels of Heaven looking at me through the eyes of a beautiful woman. I also saw the devils of hell raging in the heart of an evil man. He who does not see the angels and devils in the beauty and malice of life will be far removed from knowledge, and his spirit will be empty of affection.

6

THE HAND OF DESTINY

In the spring of that wonderful year, I was in Beirut. The gardens were full of Nisan flowers and the earth was carpeted with green grass, all like a secret of earth revealed to Heaven. The orange trees and apple trees, looking like houris or brides sent by nature to inspire poets and excite the imagination, were wearing white garments of perfumed blossoms.

Spring is beautiful everywhere, but it is most beautiful in Lebanon. It is a spirit that roams round the earth but hovers over Lebanon, conversing with kings and prophets, singing with the rivers the songs of Solomon, and repeating with the Holy Cedars of Lebanon the memory of ancient glory. Beirut, free from the mud of winter and the dust of summer, is like a bride in the spring, or like a mermaid sitting by the side of a brook drying her smooth skin in the rays of the sun.

One day, in the month of Nisan, I went to visit a friend whose home was at some distance from the glamorous city. As we were conversing, a dignified man of about sixty-five entered the house. As I rose to greet him, my friend introduced him to me as Farris Effandi Karamy and then gave him my name with flattering words. The old man looked at me a moment, touching his forehead with the ends of his fingers as if he were trying to regain his memory. Then he smilingly approached me, saying, "You are the son of a very dear friend of mine, and I am happy to see that friend in your person."

Much affected by his words, I was attracted to him like a bird whose instinct leads him to his nest before the coming of the tempest. As we sat down, he told us about his friendship with my father, recalling the time which they spent together. An old man likes to return in memory to the days of his youth like a stranger who longs to go back to his own country. He delights to tell stories of the past like a poet who takes pleasure in reciting his best poem. He lives spiritually in the past because the present passes swiftly, and the future seems to him an approach to the oblivion of the grave. An hour full of old memories passed like the shadows of the trees over the grass. When Farris Effandi started to leave, he put his left hand on my shoulder and shook my right hand, saying, "I have not seen your father for twenty years. I hope you will take his place in frequent visits to my house." I promised gratefully to do my duty toward a dear friend of my father.

When the old man left the house, I asked my friend to tell me more about him. He said, "I do not know any other man in Beirut whose wealth has made him kind and whose kindness has made him wealthy. He is one of the few who come to this world and leave it without harming anyone, but people of that kind are usually miserable and oppressed because they are not clever enough to save themselves from the crookedness of others. Farris Effandi has one daughter whose character is similar to his and whose beauty and gracefulness are beyond description, and she will also be miserable because her father's wealth is placing her already at the edge of a horrible precipice."

As he uttered these words, I noticed that his face clouded. Then he continued, "Farris Effandi is a good old man with a noble heart, but he lacks will power. People lead him like a blind man. His daughter obeys him in spite of her pride and intelligence, and this is the secret which lurks in the life of father and daughter. This secret was discovered by an evil man who is a bishop and whose wickedness hides in the shadow of his Gospel. He makes the people believe that he is kind and noble. He is the head of religion in this land of the religious. The people obey and worship him. He leads them like a flock of lambs to the slaughter house. This bishop has a nephew who is full of hatefulness and corruption. The day will come sooner or later when he will place his nephew on his right and Farris Effandi's daughter on his left, and, holding with his evil hand the wreath of matrimony over their heads, will tie a pure virgin to a filthy degenerate, placing the heart of the day in the bosom of night.

"That is all I can tell you about Farris Effandi and his daughter, so do not ask me any more questions."

Saying this, he turned his head toward the window as if he were trying to solve the problems of human existence by concentrating on the beauty of the universe.

As I left the house, I told my friend that I was going to visit Farris Effandi in a few days for the purpose of fulfilling my promise and for the sake of the friendship which had joined him and my father. He stared at me for a moment, and I noticed a change in his expression as if my few simple words had revealed to him a new idea. Then he looked straight through my eyes in a strange manner, a look of love, mercy, and fear—the look of a prophet who foresees what no one else can divine. Then his lips trembled a little, but he said nothing when I started toward the door. That strange look followed me, the meaning of which I could not understand until I grew up in the world of experience, where hearts understand each other intuitively and where spirits are mature with knowledge.

7

The Tempest

One day Farris Effandi invited me to dinner at his home. I accepted, my spirit hungry for the divine bread which Heaven placed in the hands of Selma, the spiritual bread which makes our hearts hungrier the more we eat of it. It was this bread which Kais, the Arabian poet, Dante, and Sappho tasted and which set their hearts afire; the bread which the Goddess prepares with the sweetness of kisses and the bitterness of tears.

As I reached the home of Farris Effandi, I saw Selma sitting on a bench in the garden resting her head against a tree and looking like a bride in her white silk dress, or like a sentinel guarding that place.

Silently and reverently I approached and sat by her. I could not talk; so I resorted to silence, the only language of the heart, but I felt that Selma was listening to my wordless call and watching the ghost of my soul in my eyes.

In a few minutes the old man came out and greeted me as usual. When he stretched his hand toward me, I felt as if he were blessing the secrets that united me and his daughter. Then he said, "Dinner is ready, my children; let us eat." We rose and followed him, and Selma's eyes brightened; for a new sentiment had been added to her love by her father's calling us his children.

We sat at the table enjoying the food and sipping the old wine, but our souls were living in a world far away. We were dreaming of the future and its hardships.

Three persons were separated in thoughts, but united in love; three innocent people with much feeling but little knowledge; a drama was being performed by an old man who loved his daughter and cared for her happiness, a young woman of twenty looking into the future with anxiety, and a young man, dreaming and worrying, who had tasted neither the wine of life nor its vinegar, and trying to reach the height of love and knowledge but unable to lift himself up. We three sitting in twilight were eating and drinking in that solitary home, guarded by Heaven's eyes, but at the bottoms of our glasses were hidden bitterness and anguish.

As we finished eating, one of the maids announced the presence of a man at the door who wished to see Farris Effandi. "Who is he?" asked the old man. "The Bishop's messenger," said the maid. There was a moment of silence during which Farris Effandi stared at his daughter like a prophet who gazes at Heaven to divine its secret. Then he said to the maid, "Let the man in."

As the maid left, a man, dressed in oriental uniform and with a big mustache curled at the ends, entered and greeted the old man, saying, "His Grace, the Bishop, has sent me for you with his private carriage; he wishes to discuss important business with you." The old man's face clouded and his smile disappeared. After a moment of deep thought he came close to me and said in a friendly voice, "I hope to find you here when I come back, for Selma will enjoy your company in this solitary place."

Saying this, he turned to Selma and, smiling, asked her if she agreed. She nodded her head, but her cheeks became red, and with a voice sweeter than the music of a lyre she said, "I will do my best. Father, to make our guest happy."

Selma watched the carriage that had taken her father and the Bishop's messenger until it disappeared. Then she came and sat opposite me on a divan covered with green silk. She looked like a lily bent to the carpet of green grass by the breeze of dawn. It was the will of Heaven that I should be with Selma alone, at night, in her beautiful home surrounded by trees, where silence, love, beauty, and virtue dwelt together.

We were both silent, each waiting for the other to speak, but speech is not the only means of understanding between two souls. It is not the syllables that come from the lips and tongues that bring hearts together.

There is something greater and purer than what the mouth utters. Silence illuminates our souls, whispers to our hearts, and brings them together. Silence separates us from ourselves, makes us sail the firmament of spirit, and brings us closer to Heaven; it makes us feel that bodies are no more than prisons and that this world is only a place of exile.

Selma looked at me and her eyes revealed the secret of her heart. Then she quietly said, "Let us go to the garden and sit under the trees and watch the moon come up behind the mountains." Obediently I rose from my seat, but I hesitated.

"Don't you think we had better stay here until the moon has risen and illuminates the garden?" And I continued, "The darkness hides the trees and flowers. We can see nothing."

Then she said, "If darkness hides the trees and flowers from our eyes, it will not hide love from our hearts."

Uttering these words in a strange tone, she turned her

eyes and looked through the window. I remained silent, pondering her words, weighing the true meaning of each syllable. Then she looked at me as if she regretted what she had said and tried to take away those words from my ears by the magic of her eyes. But those eyes, instead of making me forget what she had said, repeated through the depths of my heart more clearly and effectively the sweet words which had already become graven in my memory for eternity.

Every beauty and greatness in this world is created by a single thought or emotion inside a man. Everything we see today, made by past generations, was, before its appearance, a thought in the mind of a man or an impulse in the heart of a woman. The revolutions that shed so much blood and turned men's minds toward liberty were the idea of one man who lived in the midst of thousands of men. The devastating wars which destroyed empires were a thought that existed in the mind of an individual. The supreme teachings that changed the course of humanity were the ideas of a man whose genius separated him from his environment. A single thought built the Pyramids, founded the glory of Islam, and caused the burning of the library at Alexandria.

One thought will come to you at night which will elevate you to glory or lead you to the asylum. One look from a woman's eye makes you the happiest man in the world. One word from a man's lips will make you rich or poor.

That word which Selma uttered that night arrested me between my past and future, as a boat which is anchored in the midst of the ocean. That word awakened me from the slumber of youth and solitude and set me on the stage where life and death play their parts.

The scent of flowers mingled with the breeze as we came into the garden and sat silently on a bench near a jasmine tree, listening to the breathing of sleeping nature, while in the blue sky the eyes of heaven witnessed our drama.

The moon came out from behind Mount Sunnin and shone over the coast, hills, and mountains; and we could see the villages fringing the valley like apparitions which have suddenly been conjured from nothing. We could see the beauty of all Lebanon under the silver rays of the moon.

Poets of the West think of Lebanon as a legendary place, forgotten since the passing of David and Solomon and the Prophets, as the Garden of Eden became lost after the fall of Adam and Eve. To those Western Poets, the word "Lebanon" is a poetical expression associated with a mountain whose sides are drenched with the incense of the Holy Cedars. It reminds them of the temples of copper and marble standing stern and impregnable and of a herd of deer feeding in the valleys. That night I saw Lebanon dream-like with the eyes of a poet.

Thus, the appearance of things changes according to the emotions, and thus we see magic and beauty in them, while the magic and beauty are really in ourselves.

As the rays of the moon shone on the face, neck, and arms of Selma, she looked like a statue of ivory sculptured by the fingers of some worshiper of Ishtar, goddess of beauty and love. As she looked at me, she said, "Why are you silent? Why do you not tell me something about your past?" As I gazed at her, my muteness vanished, and I opened my lips and said, "Did you not hear what I said when we came to this orchard? The spirit that hears the whispering of flowers and the singing of silence can also hear the shrieking of my soul and the clamor of my heart."

She covered her face with her hands and said in a trembling voice, "Yes, I heard you—I heard a voice coming from the bosom of night and a clamor raging in the heart of the day."

Forgetting my past, my very existence—everything but Selma—I answered her, saying, "And I heard you, too, Selma. I heard exhilarating music pulsing in the air and causing the whole universe to tremble."

Upon hearing these words, she closed her eyes and on her lips I saw a smile of pleasure mingled with sadness. She whispered softly, "Now I know that there is something higher than heaven and deeper than the ocean and stranger than life and death and time. I know now what I did not know before."

At that moment Selma became dearer than a friend and closer than a sister and more beloved than a sweetheart. She became a supreme thought, a beautiful dream, an overpowering emotion living in my spirit.

It is wrong to think that love comes from long companionship and persevering courtship. Love is the offspring of spiritual affinity and unless that affinity is created in a moment, it will not be created in years or even generations.

Then Selma raised her head and gazed at the horizon where Mount Sunnin meets the sky, and said, "Yesterday you were like a brother to me, with whom I lived and by whom I sat calmly under my father's care. Now, I feel the presence of something stranger and sweeter than brotherly affection, an unfamiliar commingling of love and fear that fills my heart with sorrow and happiness."

I responded, "This emotion which we fear and which shakes us when it passes through our hearts is the law of nature that guides the moon around the earth and the sun around God."

She put her hand on my head and wove her fingers

through my hair. Her face brightened and tears came out of her eyes like drops of dew on the leaves of a lily, and she said, "Who would believe our story—who would believe that in this hour we have surmounted the obstacles of doubt? Who would believe that the month of Nisan which brought us together for the first time, is the month that halted us in the Holy of Holies of life?"

Her hand was still on my head as she spoke, and I would not have preferred a royal crown or a wreath of glory to that beautiful smooth hand whose fingers were twined in my hair.

Then I answered her: "People will not believe our story because they do not know that love is the only flower that grows and blossoms without the aid of seasons, but was it Nisan that brought us together for the first time, and is it this hour that has arrested us in the Holy of Holies of life? Is it not the hand of God that brought our souls close together before birth and made us prisoners of each other for all the days and nights? Man's life does not commence in the womb and never ends in the grave; and this firmament, full of moonlight and stars, is not deserted by loving souls and intuitive spirits."

As she drew her hand away from my head, I felt a kind of electrical vibration at the roots of my hair mingled with the night breeze. Like a devoted worshiper who receives his blessing by kissing the altar in a shrine, I took Selma's hand, placed my burning lips on it, and gave it a long kiss, the memory of which melts my heart and awakens by its sweetness all the virtue of my spirit.

An hour passed, every minute of which was a year of love. The silence of the night, moonlight, flowers, and trees made us forget all reality except love, when suddenly we heard the galloping of horses and rattling of carriage wheels.

Awakened from our pleasant swoon and plunged from the world of dreams into the world of perplexity and misery, we found that the old man had returned from his mission. We rose and walked through the orchard to meet him.

When the carriage reached the entrance of the garden, Farris Effandi dismounted and slowly walked towards us, bending forward slightly as if he were carrying a heavy load. He approached Selma and placed both of his hands on her shoulders and stared at her. Tears coursed down his wrinkled cheeks and his lips trembled with sorrowful smile. In a choking voice, he said, "My beloved Selma, very soon you will be taken away from the arms of your father to the arms of another man. Very soon fate will carry you from this lonely home to the world's spacious court, and this garden will miss the pressure of your footsteps, and your father will become a stranger to you. All is done; may God bless you."

Hearing these words, Selma's face clouded and her eyes froze as if she felt a premonition of death. Then she screamed, like a bird shot down, suffering, and trembling, and in a choked voice said, "What do you say? What do you mean? Where are you sending me?"

Then she looked at him searchingly, trying to discover his secret. In a moment she said, "I understand. I understand everything. The Bishop has demanded me from you and has prepared a cage for this bird with broken wings. Is this your will, Father?"

His answer was a deep sigh. Tenderly he led Selma into the house while I remained standing in the garden, waves of perplexity beating upon me like a tempest upon autumn leaves. Then I followed them into the living room, and to avoid embarrassment, shook the old man's hand, looked at Selma, my beautiful star, and left the house.

As I reached the end of the garden I heard the old man calling me and turned to meet him. Apologetically he took my hand and said, "Forgive me, my son. I have ruined your evening with the shedding of tears, but please come to see me when my house is deserted and I am lonely and desperate. Youth, my dear son, does not combine with senility, as morning does not meet the night; but you will come to me and call to my memory the youthful days which I spent with your father, and you will tell me the news of life which does not count me as among its sons any longer. Will you not visit me when Selma leaves and I am left here in loneliness?"

While he said these sorrowful words and I silently shook his hand, I felt the warm tears falling from his eyes upon my hand. Trembling with sorrow and filial affection, I felt as if my heart were choked with grief. When I raised my head and he saw the tears in my eyes, he bent toward me and touched my forehead with his lips. "Good-bye, son, Good-bye."

An old man's tear is more potent than that of a young man because it is the residuum of life in his weakening body. A young man's tear is like a drop of dew on the leaf of a rose, while that of an old man is like a yellow leaf which falls with the wind at the approach of winter.

As I left the house of Farris Effandi Karamy, Selma's voice still rang in my ears, her beauty followed me like a wraith, and her father's tears dried slowly on my hand.

My departure was like Adam's exodus from Paradise, but the Eve of my heart was not with me to make the whole world an Eden. That night, in which I had been born again, I felt that I saw death's face for the first time.

Thus the sun enlivens and kills the fields with its heat.

8

The Lake of Fire

Everything that a man does secretly in the darkness of night will be clearly revealed in daylight. Words uttered in privacy will become unexpectedly common conversation. Deeds which we hide today in the corners of our lodgings will be shouted on every street tomorrow.

Thus the ghosts of darkness revealed the purpose of Bishop Bulos Galib's meeting with Farris Effandi Karamy, and his conversation was repeated all over the neighborhood until it reached my ears.

The discussion that took place between Bishop Bulos Galib and Farris Effandi that night was not over the problems of the poor or the widows and orphans. The main purpose for sending after Farris Effandi and bringing him in the Bishop's private carriage was the betrothal of Selma to the Bishop's nephew, Mansour Bey Galib.

Selma was the only child of the wealthy Farris Effandi, and the Bishop's choice fell on Selma, not on account of her beauty and noble spirit, but on account of her father's money which would guarantee Mansour Bey a good and prosperous fortune and make him an important man.

The heads of religion in the East are not satisfied with their own munificence, but they must strive to make all members of their families superiors and oppressors. The glory of a prince goes to his eldest son by inheritance, but the exaltation of a religious head is contagious among his brothers and nephews. Thus the Christian bishop and the Moslem imam and the Brahman priest become like sea reptiles who clutch their prey with many tentacles and suck their blood with numerous mouths.

When the Bishop demanded Selma's hand for his nephew, the only answer that he received from her father was deep silence and falling tears, for he hated to lose his only child. Any man's soul trembles when he is separated from his only daughter whom he has reared to young womanhood.

The sorrow of parents at the marriage of a daughter is equal to their happiness at the marriage of a son, because a son brings to the family a new member, while a daughter, upon her marriage, is lost to them.

Farris Effandi perforce granted the Bishop's request, obeying his will unwillingly, because Farris Effandi knew the Bishop's nephew very well, knew that he was dangerous, full of hate, wickedness, and corruption.

In Lebanon, no Christian could oppose his bishop and remain in good standing. No man could disobey his religious head and keep his reputation. The eye could not resist a spear without being pierced, and the hand could not grasp a sword without being cut off.

Suppose that Farris Effandi had resisted the Bishop and refused his wish; then Selma's reputation would have been ruined and her name would have been blemished by the dirt of lips and tongues. In the opinion of the fox, high bunches of grapes that can't be reached are sour.

Thus destiny seized Selma and led her like a humiliated slave in the procession of miserable oriental woman, and thus fell that noble spirit into the trap after having flown freely on the white wings of love in a sky full of moonlight scented with the odor of flowers.

In some countries, the parents' wealth is a source of misery for the children. The wide strong box which the father and mother together have used for the safety of their wealth becomes a narrow, dark prison for the souls of their heirs. The Almighty Dinar* which the people worship becomes a demon which punishes the spirit and deadens the heart. Selma Karamy was one of those who were victims of their parents' wealth and bridegrooms' cupidity. Had it not been for her father's wealth, Selma would still be living happily.

A week had passed. The love of Selma was my sole entertainer, singing songs of happiness for me at night and waking me at dawn to reveal the meaning of life and the secrets of nature. It is a heavenly love that is free from jealousy, rich and never harmful to the spirit. It is a deep affinity that bathes the soul in contentment; a deep hunger for affection which, when satisfied, fills the soul with bounty; a tenderness that creates hope without agitating the soul, changing earth to paradise and life to a sweet and beautiful dream. In the morning, when I walked in the fields, I saw the token of Eternity in the awakening of nature, and when I sat by the seashore I heard the waves singing the song of Eternity. And when I walked in the streets I saw the beauty of life and the splendor of humanity in the appearance of passers-by and movements of workers.

Those days passed like ghosts and disappeared like clouds, and soon nothing was left for me but sorrowful memories. The eyes with which I used to look at the beauty

*Kind of money used in the Near East.

of spring and the awakening of nature, could see nothing but the fury of the tempest and the misery of winter. The ears with which I formerly heard with delight the song of the waves, could hear only the howling of the wind and the wrath of the sea against the precipice. The soul which had observed happily the tireless vigor of mankind and the glory of the universe, was tortured by the knowledge of disappointment and failure. Nothing was more beautiful than those days of love, and nothing was more bitter than those horrible nights of sorrow.

When I could no longer resist the impulse, I went, on the weekend, once more to Selma's home—the shrine which Beauty had erected and which Love had blessed, in which the spirit could worship and the heart kneel humbly and pray. When I entered the garden I felt a power pulling me away from this world and placing me in a sphere supernaturally free from struggle and hardship. Like a mystic who receives a revelation of Heaven, I saw myself amid the trees and flowers, and as I approached the entrance of the house I beheld Selma sitting on the bench in the shadow of a jasmine tree where we both had sat the week before, on that night which Providence had chosen for the beginning of my happiness and sorrow.

She neither moved nor spoke as I approached her. She seemed to have known intuitively that I was coming, and when I sat by her she gazed at me for a moment and sighed deeply, then turned her head and looked at the sky. And, after a moment full of magic silence, she turned back toward me and tremblingly took my hand and said in a faint voice, "Look at me, my friend; study my face and read in it that which you want to know and which I can not recite. Look at me, my beloved... look at me, my brother."

I gazed at her intently and saw that those eyes, which

a few days ago were smiling like lips and moving like the wings of a nightingale, were already sunken and glazed with sorrow and pain. Her face, that had resembled the unfolding, sunkissed leaves of a lily, had faded and become colorless. Her sweet lips were like two withering roses that autumn has left on their stems. Her neck, that had been a column of ivory, was bent forward as if it no longer could support the burden of grief in her head.

All these changes I saw in Selma's face, but to me they were like a passing cloud that covered the face of the moon and makes it more beautiful. A look which reveals inward stress adds more beauty to the face, no matter how much tragedy and pain it bespeaks; but the face which, in silence, does not announce hidden mysteries is not beautiful, regardless of the symmetry of its features. The cup does not entice our lips unless the wine's color is seen through the transparent crystal.

Selma, on that evening, was like a cup full of heavenly wine concocted of the bitterness and sweetness of life. Unaware, she symbolized the oriental woman who never leaves her parents' home until she puts upon her neck the heavy yoke of her husband, who never leaves her loving mother's arms until she must live as a slave, enduring the harshness of her husband's mother.

I continued to look at Selma and listen to her depressed spirit and suffer with her until I felt that time had ceased and the universe had faded from existence. I could see only her two large eyes staring fixedly at me and could feel only her cold, trembling hand holding mine.

I woke from my swoon hearing Selma saying quietly, "Come, my beloved, let us discuss the horrible future before it comes. My father has just left the house to see the man who is going to be my companion until death. My father, whom God chose for the purpose of my existence, will meet the man whom the world has selected to be my master for the rest of my life. In the heart of this city, the old man who accompanied me during my youth will meet the young man who will be my companion for the coming years. Tonight the two families will set the marriage date. What a strange and impressive hour! Last week at this time, under this jasmine tree, Love embraced my soul for the first time, while Destiny was writing the first word of my life's story at the Bishop's mansion. Now, while my father and my suitor are planning the day of marriage, I see your spirit quivering around me as a thirsty bird flickers above a spring of water guarded by a hungry serpent. Oh, how great this night is! And how deep is its mystery!"

Hearing these words, I felt that the dark ghost of complete despondency was seizing our love to choke it in its infancy, and I answered her, "That bird will remain flickering over that spring until thirst destroys him or falls into the grasp of a serpent and becomes its prey."

She responded, "No, my beloved, this nightingale should remain alive and sing until dark comes, until spring passes, until the end of the world, and keep on singing eternally. His voice should not be silenced, because he brings life to my heart, his wings should not be broken, because their motion removes the cloud from my heart."

Then I whispered, "Selma, my beloved, thirst will exhaust him; and fear will kill him."

She replied immediately with trembling lips, "The thirst of soul is sweeter than the wine of material things, and the fear of spirit is dearer than the security of the body. But listen, my beloved, listen carefully, I am standing today at the door of a new life which I know nothing about. I am like a blind man who feels his way so that he will not fall. My father's wealth has placed me in the slave market, and this man has bought me. I neither know nor love him, but I shall learn to love him, and I shall obey him, serve him, and make him happy. I shall give him all that a weak woman can give a strong man.

"But you, my beloved, are still in the prime of life. You can walk freely upon life's spacious path, carpeted with flowers. You are free to traverse the world, making of your heart a torch to light your way. You can think, talk, and act freely; you can write your name on the face of life because you are a man; you can live as a master because your father's wealth will not place you in the slave market to be bought and sold; you can marry the woman of your choice and, before she lives in your home, you can let her reside in your heart and can exchange confidences without hindrance."

Silence prevailed for a moment, and Selma continued, "But, is it now that Life will tear us apart so that you may attain the glory of a man and I the duty of a woman? Is it for this that the valley swallows the song of the nightingale in its depths, and the wind scatters the petals of the rose, and the feet tread upon the wine cup? Were all those nights we spent in the moonlight by the jasmine tree, where our souls united, in vain? Did we fly swiftly toward the stars until our wings tired, and are we descending now into the abyss? Or was Love asleep when he came to us, and did he, when he woke, become angry and decide to punish us? Or did our spirits turn the night's breeze into a wind that tore us to pieces and blew us like dust to the depth of the valley? We disobeyed no commandment, nor did we taste of forbidden fruit, so what is making us leave this paradise? We never conspired or practiced mutiny, then why are we descending to hell? No, no, the moments which united us are greater than centuries, and the light that illuminated our spirits is stronger than the dark; and if the tempest separates us on this rough ocean, the waves will unite us on the calm shore; and if this life kills us, death will unite us. A woman's heart will not change with time or season; even if it dies eternally, it will never perish. A woman's heart is like a field turned into a battleground; after the trees are uprooted and the grass is burned and the rocks are reddened with blood and the earth is planted with bones and skulls, it is calm and silent as if nothing has happened; for the spring and autumn come at their intervals and resume their work.

"And now, my beloved, what shall we do? How shall we part and when shall we meet? Shall we consider love a strange visitor who came in the evening and left us in the morning? Or shall we suppose this affection a dream that came in our sleep and departed when we awoke?

"Shall we consider this week an hour of intoxication to be replaced by soberness? Raise your head and let me look at you, my beloved; open your lips and let me hear your voice. Speak to me! Will you remember me after this tempest has sunk the ship of our love? Will you hear the whispering of my wings in the silence of the night? Will you hear my spirit fluttering over you? Will you listen to my sighs? Will you see my shadow approach with the shadows of dusk and disappear with the flush of dawn? Tell me, my beloved, what will you be after having been magic ray to my eyes, sweet song to my ears, and wings to my soul? What will you be?"

Hearing these words, my heart melted, and I answered her, "I will be as you want me to be, my beloved."

Then she said, "I want you to love me as a poet loves his sorrowful thoughts. I want you to remember me as a traveler remembers a calm pool in which his image was reflected as he drank its water. I want you to remember me as a mother remembers her child that died before it saw the light, and I want you to remember me as a merciful king remembers a prisoner who died before his pardon reached him. I want you to be my companion, and I want you to visit my father and console him in his solitude because I shall be leaving him soon and shall be a stranger to him."

I answered her, saying, "I will do all you have said and will make my soul an envelope for your soul, and my heart a residence for your beauty and my breast a grave for your sorrows. I shall love you, Selma, as the prairies love the spring, and I shall live in you the life of a flower under the sun's rays. I shall sing your name as the valley sings the echo of the bells of the village churches; I shall listen to the language of your soul as the shore listens to the story of the waves. I shall remember you as a stranger remembers his beloved country, and as a hungry man remembers a banquet, and as a dethroned king remembers the days of his glory, and as a prisoner remembers the hours of ease and freedom. I shall remember you as a sower remembers the bundles of wheat on his threshing floor, and as a shepherd remembers the green prairies and sweet brooks."

Selma listened to my words with palpitating heart, and said, "Tomorrow the truth will become ghostly and the awakening will be like a dream. Will a lover be satisfied embracing a ghost, or will a thirsty man quench his thirst from the spring of a dream?"

I answered her, "Tomorrow, destiny will put you in the midst of a peaceful family, but it will send me into the world of struggle and warfare. You will be in the home of a person whom chance has made most fortunate through your beauty and virtue, while I shall be living a life of suffering and fear. You will enter the gate of life, while I shall enter the gate of death. You will be received hospitably, while I shall exist in solitude, but I shall erect a statue of love and worship it in the valley of death. Love will be my sole comforter, and I shall drink love like wine and wear it like a garment. At dawn, Love will wake me from slumber and take me to the distant field, and at noon will lead me to the shadows of trees, where I will find shelter with the birds from the heat of the sun. In the evening, it will cause me to pause before sunset to hear nature's farewell song to the light of day and will show me ghostly clouds sailing in the sky. At night, Love will embrace me, and I shall sleep, dreaming of the heavenly world where the spirits of lovers and poets abide. In the Spring I shall walk side by side with love among violets and jasmines and drink the remaining drops of winter in the lily cups. In Summer we shall make the bundles of hay our pillows and the grass our bed, and the blue sky will cover us as we gaze at the stars and moon.

"In Autumn, Love and I will go to the vineyard and sit by the wine press and watch the grapevines being denuded of their golden ornaments, and the migrating flocks of birds will wing over us. In Winter we shall sit by the fireside reciting stories of long ago and chronicles of far countries. During my youth, Love will be my teacher; in middle age, my help; and in old age, my delight. Love, my beloved Selma, will stay with me to the end of my life, and after death the hand of God will unite us again."

All these words came from the depths of my heart like flames of fire which leap raging from the hearth and then disappear in the ashes. Selma was weeping as if her eyes were lips answering me with tears.

Those whom love has not given wings cannot fly behind the cloud of appearances to see the magic world in which Selma's spirit and mine existed together in that sorrowfully happy hour. Those whom Love has not chosen as followers do not hear when Love calls. This story is not for them. Even if they should comprehend these pages, they would not be able to grasp the shadowy meanings which are not clothed in words and do not reside on paper, but what human being is he who has never sipped the wine from the cup of love, and what spirit is it that has never stood reverently before that lighted altar in the temple whose pavement is the hearts of men and women and whose ceiling is the secret canopy of dreams? What flower is that on whose leaves the dawn has never poured a drop of dew; what streamlet is that which lost its course without going to the sea?

Selma raised her face toward the sky and gazed at the heavenly stars which studded the firmament. She stretched out her hands; her eyes widened, and her lips trembled. On her pale face, I could see the signs of sorrow, oppression, hopelessness, and pain. Then she cried, "Oh, Lord, what has a woman done that hath offended Thee? What sin has she committed to deserve such a punishment? For what crime has she been awarded everlasting castigation? Oh, Lord, Thou art strong, and I am weak. Why hast Thou made me suffer pain? Thou art great and almighty, while I am nothing but a tiny creature crawling before Thy throne. Why hast Thou crushed me with Thy foot? Thou art a raging tempest, and I am like dust; why, my Lord, hast Thou flung me upon the cold earth? Thou art powerful, and I am helpless; why art Thou fighting me? Thou art considerate, and I am prudent; why art Thou destroying me? Thou hast created woman with love, and why, with love, dost Thou ruin her? With Thy right hand dost Thou lift her, and with Thy left hand dost Thou strike her into the abyss, and she knows not why. In her mouth Thou blowest the breath of life, and in her heart Thou sowest the seeds of death. Thou dost show her the path of happiness, but Thou leadest her in the road of misery; in her mouth Thou dost place a song of happiness, but then Thou dost close her lips with sorrow and dost fetter her tongue with agony. With Thy mysterious fingers dost Thou dress her wounds, and with Thine hands Thou drawest the dread of pain round her pleasures. In her bed Thou hidest pleasure and peace, but beside it Thou dost erect obstacles and fear. Thou dost excite her affection through Thy will, and from her affection does shame emanate. By Thy will Thou showest her the beauty of creation, but her love for beauty becomes a terrible famine. Thou dost make her drink life in the cup of death, and death in the cup of life. Thou purifiest her with tears, and in tears her life streams away. Oh, Lord, Thou hast opened my eyes with love, and with love Thou hast blinded me. Thou hast kissed me with Thy lips and struck me with Thy strong hand. Thou hast planted in my heart a white rose, but around the rose a barrier of thorns. Thou hast tied my present with the spirit of a young man whom I love, but my life with the body of an unknown man. So help me, my Lord, to be strong in this deadly struggle and assist me to be truthful and virtuous until death. Thy will be done, Oh, Lord God."

Silence continued. Selma looked down, pale and frail; her arms dropped, and her head bowed and it seemed to me as if a tempest had broken a branch from a tree and cast it down to dry and perish.

I took her cold hand and kissed it, but when I attempted to console her, it was I who needed consolation more than she did. I kept silent, thinking of our plight and listening to my heartbeats. Neither of us said more.

Extreme torture is mute, and so we sat silent, petrified, like columns of marble buried under the sand of an earthquake. Neither wished to listen to the other because our heart-threads had become weak and even breathing would have broken them.

It was midnight, and we could see the crescent moon rising from behind Mt. Sunnin, and it looked, in the midst of the stars, like the face of a corpse, in a coffin surrounded by the dim lights of candles. And Lebanon looked like an old man whose back was bent with age and whose eyes were a haven for insomnia, watching the dark and waiting for dawn, like a king sitting on the ashes of his throne in the debris of his palace.

The mountains, trees, and rivers change their appearance with the vicissitudes of times and seasons, as a man changes with his experiences and emotions. The lofty poplar that resembles a bride in the daytime, will look like a column of smoke in the evening; the huge rock that stands impregnable at noon, will appear to be a miserable pauper at night, with earth for his bed and the sky for his cover; and the rivulet that we see glittering in the morning and hear singing the hymn of Eternity, will, in the evening, turn to a stream of tears wailing like a mother bereft of her child, and Lebanon, that had looked dignified a week before, when the moon was full and our spirits were happy, looked sorrowful and lonesome that night.

We stood up and bade each other farewell, but love and despair stood between us like two ghosts, one stretching his wings with his fingers over our throats, one weeping and the other laughing hideously.

As I took Selma's hand and put it to my lips, she came close to me and placed a kiss on my forehead, then dropped on the wooden bench. She shut her eyes and whispered softly, "Oh, Lord God, have mercy on me and mend my broken wings!"

As I left Selma in the garden, I felt as if my senses were

covered with a thick veil, like a lake whose surface is concealed by fog.

The beauty of trees, the moonlight, the deep silence, everything about me looked ugly and horrible. The true light that had showed me the beauty and wonder of the universe was converted to a great flame of fire that seared my heart; and the Eternal music I used to hear became a clamor, more frightening than the roar of a lion.

I reached my room, and like a wounded bird shot down by a hunter, I fell on my bed, repeating the words of Selma: "Oh, Lord God, have mercy on me and mend my broken wings!"

9

The Sacrifice

One day in the late part of June, as the people left the city for the mountain to avoid the heat of summer, I went as usual to the temple to meet Selma, carrying with me a little book of Andalusian poems. As I reached the temple I sat there waiting for Selma, glancing at intervals at the pages of my book, reciting those verses which filled my heart with ecstasy and brought to my soul the memory of the kings, poets, and knights who bade farewell to Granada, and left, with tears in their eyes and sorrow in their hearts, their palaces, institutions and hopes behind. In an hour I saw Selma walking in the midst of the gardens and approaching the temple, leaning on her parasol as if she were carrying all the worries of the world upon her shoulders. As she entered the temple and sat by me, I noticed some sort of change in her eyes and I was anxious to inquire about it.

Selma felt what was going on in my mind, and she put her hand on my head and said, "Come close to me, come my beloved, come and let me quench my thirst, for the hour of separation has come."

I asked her, "Did your husband find out about our meetings here?" She responded, "My husband does not care about me, neither does he know how I spend my time, for he is busy with those poor girls whom poverty has driven into the houses of ill fame; those girls who sell their bodies for bread, kneaded with blood and tears."

I inquired, "What prevents you from coming to this temple and sitting by me reverently before God? Is your soul requesting our separation?"

She answered with tears in her eyes, "No, my beloved, my spirit did not ask for separation, for you are a part of me. My eyes never get tired of looking at you, for you are their light; but if destiny ruled that I should walk the rough path of life loaded with shackles, would I be satisfied if your fate should be like mine?" Then she added, "I cannot say everything, because the tongue is mute with pain and cannot talk; the lips are sealed with misery and cannot move; all I can say to you is that I am afraid you may fall in the same trap I fell in."

Then I asked, "What do you mean, Selma, and of whom are you afraid?" She covered her face with her hands and said, "The Bishop has already found out that once a month I have been leaving the grave which he buried me in."

I inquired, "Did the Bishop find out about our meetings here?" She answered, "If he did, you would not see me here sitting by you; but he is getting suspicious and he informed all his servants and guards to watch me closely. I am feeling that the house I live in and the path I walk on are all eyes watching me, and fingers pointing at me, and ears listening to the whisper of my thoughts."

She was silent for a while, and then she added, with tears pouring down her cheeks, "I am not afraid of the Bishop, for wetness does not scare the drowned, but I am afraid you might fall into the trap and become his prey; you are still young and free as the sunlight. I am not frightened of fate which has shot all its arrows in my breast, but I am afraid the serpent might bite your feet and detain you from climbing the mountain peak where the future awaits you with its pleasure and glory."

I said, "He who has not been bitten by the serpents of light and snapped at by the wolves of darkness will always be deceived by the days and nights. But listen, Selma, listen carefully; is separation the only means of avoiding people's evils and meanness? Has the path of love and freedom been closed and is nothing left except submission to the will of the slaves of death?"

She responded, "Nothing is left save separation and bidding each other farewell."

With rebellious spirit I took her hand and said excitedly, "We have yielded to the people's will for a long time; since the time we met until this hour we have been led by the blind and have worshipped with them before their idols. Since the time I met you we have been in the hands of the Bishop like two balls which he has thrown around as he pleased. Are we going to submit to his will until death takes us away? Did God give us the breath of life to place it under death's feet? Did He give us liberty to make it a shadow for slavery? He who extinguishes his spirit's fire with his own hands is an infidel in the eyes of Heaven, for Heaven set the fire that burns in our spirits. He who does not rebel against oppression is doing himself injustice. I love you, Selma, and you love me, too; and Love is a precious treasure, it is God's gift to sensitive and great spirits. Shall we throw this treasure away and let the pigs scatter it and trample on it? This world is full of wonder and beauty. Why are we living in this narrow tunnel which the Bishop and his assistants have dug out for us? Life is full of happiness and freedom; why don't we take this heavy yoke off our shoulders and break the chains tied to our feet, and walk freely toward peace? Get up and let us leave this small temple for God's great temple. Let us leave this country and all its slavery and ignorance for another country far away and unreached by the hands of the thieves. Let us go to the coast under the cover of night and catch a boat that will take us across the oceans, where we can find a new life full of happiness and understanding. Do not hesitate, Selma, for these minutes are more precious to us than the crowns of kings and more sublime than the thrones of angels. Let us follow the column of light that leads us from this arid desert into the green fields where flowers and aromatic plants grow."

She shook her head and gazed at something invisible on the ceiling of the temple; a sorrowful smile appeared on her lips; then she said, "No, no my beloved. Heaven placed in my hand a cup, full of vinegar and gall; I forced myself to drink it in order to know the full bitterness at the bottom until nothing was left save a few drops, which I shall drink patiently. I am not worthy of a new life of love and peace; I am not strong enough for life's pleasure and sweetness, because a bird with broken wings cannot fly in the spacious sky. The eyes that are accustomed to the dim light of a candle are not strong enough to stare at the sun. Do not talk to me of happiness; its memory makes me suffer. Mention not peace to me; its shadow frightens me; but look at me and I will show you the holy torch which Heaven has lighted in the ashes of my heart—you know that I love you as a mother loves her only child, and Love only taught me to protect you even from myself. It is Love, purified with fire, that stops me from following you to the farthest land. Love kills my desires so that you may live freely and virtuously. Limited love asks for possession of the beloved, but the unlimited asks only for itself. Love that comes between the naiveté and awakening of youth satisfies itself with possessing, and grows with embraces. But Love which is born in the firmament's lap and has descended with the night's secrets is not contented with anything but Eternity and immortality; it does not stand reverently before anything except deity.

"When I knew that the Bishop wanted to stop me from leaving his nephew's house and to take my only pleasure away from me, I stood before the window of my room and looked toward the sea, thinking of the vast countries beyond it and the real freedom and personal independence which can be found there. I felt that I was living close to you, surrounded by the shadow of your spirit, submerged in the ocean of your affection. But all these thoughts which illuminate a woman's heart and make her rebel against old customs and live in the shadow of freedom and justice, made me believe that I am weak and that our love is limited and feeble, unable to stand before the sun's face. I cried like a king whose kingdom and treasures have been usurped, but immediately I saw your face through my tears and your eyes gazing at me and I remembered what you said to me once *(Come, Selma, come and let us be strong towers before the tempest. Let us stand like brave soldiers before the enemy and face his weapons. If we are killed, we shall die as martyrs; and if we win, we shall live as heroes. Braving obstacles and hardships is nobler than retreat to tranquility.)* These words, my beloved, you uttered when the wings of death were hovering around my father's bed; I remembered them yesterday when the wings of despair were hovering above my head. I strengthened myself and felt, while in the darkness of my prison, some sort of precious freedom easing our difficulties and diminishing our sorrows. I found out that our love was as deep as the ocean and as high as the stars and as spacious as the sky. I came here to see you, and in my weak spirit there is a new strength, and this strength is the ability to sacrifice a great thing in order to obtain a greater one; it is the sacrifice of my happiness so that you may remain virtuous and honorable in the eyes of the people and be far away from their treachery and persecution...

"In the past, when I came to this place I felt as if heavy chains were pulling down on me, but today I came here with a new determination that laughs at the shackles and shortens the way. I used to come to this temple like a scared phantom, but today I came like a brave woman who feels the urgency of sacrifice and knows the value of suffering, a woman who likes to protect the one she loves from the ignorant people and from her hungry spirit. I used to sit by you like a trembling shadow, but today I came here to show you my true self before Ishtar and Christ.

"I am a tree, grown in the shade, and today I stretched my branches to tremble for a while in the daylight. I came here to tell you good-bye, my beloved, and it is my hope that our farewell will be great and awful like our love. Let our farewell be like fire that bends the gold and makes it more resplendent."

Selma did not allow me to speak or protest, but she looked at me, her eyes glittering, her face remaining its dignity, seeming like an angel worthy of silence and respect. Then she flung herself upon me, something which she had never done before, and put her smooth arms around me and printed a long, deep, fiery kiss on my lips.

As the sun went down, withdrawing its rays from those gardens and orchards, Selma moved to the middle of the temple and gazed long at its walls and corners as if she wanted to pour the light of her eyes on its pictures and symbols. Then she walked forward and reverently knelt before the picture of Christ and kissed His feet, and she whispered, "Oh, Christ, I have chosen Thy Cross and deserted Ishtar's world of pleasure and happiness; I have worn the wreath of thorns and discarded the wreath of laurel and washed myself with blood and tears instead of perfume and scent; I have drunk vinegar and gall from a cup which was meant for wine and nectar; accept me, my Lord, among Thy followers and lead me toward Galilee with those who have chosen Thee, contented with their sufferings and delighted with their sorrows."

Then she rose and looked at me and said, "Now I shall return happily to my dark cave, where horrible ghosts reside. Do not sympathize with me, my beloved, and do not feel sorry for me, because the soul that sees the shadow of God once will never be frightened, thereafter, of the ghosts of devils. And the eye that looks on Heaven once will not be closed by the pains of the world."

Uttering these words, Selma left the place of worship; and I remained there lost in a deep sea of thoughts, absorbed in the world of revelation where God sits on the throne and the angels write down the acts of human beings, and the souls recite the tragedy of life, and the brides of Heaven sing the hymns of love, sorrow and immortality.

Night had already come when I awakened from my swoon and found myself bewildered in the midst of the gardens, repeating the echo of every word uttered by Selma and remembering her silence, her actions, her movements, her expressions and the touch of her hands, until I realized the meaning of farewell and the pain of lonesomeness. I was depressed and heart-broken. It was my first discovery of the fact that men, even if they are born free, will remain slaves of strict laws enacted by their forefathers; and that the firmament, which we imagine as unchanging, is the yielding of today to the will of tomorrow and submission of yesterday to the will of today—Many a time, since that night, I have thought of the spiritual law which made Selma prefer death to life, and many a time I have made a comparison between nobility of sacrifice and happiness of rebellion to find out which one is nobler and more beautiful; but until now I have distilled only one truth out of the whole matter, and this truth is *sincerity*, which makes all our deeds beautiful and honorable. And this *sincerity* was in Selma Karamy.

10

THE CREATION

The God separated a spirit from Himself and fashioned it into beauty. He showered upon her all the blessings of gracefulness and kindness. He gave her the cup of happiness and said, "Drink not from this cup unless you forget the past and the future, for happiness is naught but the moment." And He also gave her a cup of sorrow and said, "Drink from this cup and you will understand the meaning of the fleeting instants of the joy of life for sorrow ever abounds."

And the God bestowed upon her a love that would desert her forever upon her first sigh of earthly satisfaction, and a sweetness that would banish with her first awareness of flattery.

And He gave her wisdom from heaven to lead her to the all-righteous path, and placed in the depth of her heart an eye that sees the unseen, and created in her an affection and goodness toward all things. He dressed her with raiment of hopes spun by the angels of heaven from the sinews of the rainbow. And He cloaked her in the shadow of confusion, which is the dawn of life and light.

Then the God took consuming fire from the furnace of anger, and searing wind from the desert of ignorance, and sharp-cutting sands from the shore of selfishness, and coarse earth from under the feet of ages, and combined them all and fashioned Man. He gave to Man a blind power that rages and drives him into a madness which extinguishes only before gratification of desire, and placed life in him which is the specter of death.

And the God laughed and cried. He felt an overwhelming love and pity for Man, and sheltered him beneath His guidance.

11

PEACE

The tempest calmed after bending the branches of the trees and leaning heavily upon the grain in the field. The stars appeared as broken remnants of the lightning, but now silence prevailed over all, as if Nature's war had never been fought.

At that hour a young woman entered her chamber and knelt by her bed sobbing bitterly. Her heart flamed with agony but she could finally open her lips and say, "Oh Lord, bring him home safely to me. I have exhausted my tears and can offer no more, oh Lord, full of love and mercy. My patience is drained and calamity is seeking possession of my heart. Save him, oh Lord, from the iron paws of War; deliver him from such unmerciful Death, for he is weak, governed by the strong. Oh Lord, save my beloved, who is thine own son, from the foe, who is thy foe. Keep him from the forced pathway to Death's door; let him see me, or come and take me to him."

Quietly a young man entered. His head was wrapped in bandage soaked with escaping life.

He approached her with a greeting of tears and laughter, then took her hand and placed against it his flaming lips. And with a voice which bespoke past sorrow, and joy of union, and uncertainty of her reaction, he said, "Fear me not, for I am the object of your plea. Be glad, for Peace has carried me back safely to you, and humanity has restored what greed essayed to take from us. Be not sad, but smile, my beloved. Do not express bewilderment, for Love has power that dispels Death; charm that conquers the enemy. I am your one. Think me not a specter emerging from the House of Death to visit your Home of Beauty.

"Do not be frightened, for I am now Truth, spared from swords and fire to reveal to the people the triumph of Love over War. I am Word uttering introduction to the play of happiness and peace."

Then the young man became speechless and his tears spoke the language of the heart; and the angels of Joy hovered about that dwelling, and the two hearts restored the singleness which had been taken from them.

At dawn the two stood in the middle of the field, contemplating the beauty of Nature injured by the tempest. After a deep and comforting silence, the soldier looked to the east and said to his sweetheart, "Look at the Darkness, giving birth to the Sun."

12

Song of the Soul

In the depth of my soul there is
A wordless song—a song that lives
In the seed of my heart.
It refuses to melt with ink on
Parchment; it engulfs my affection
In a transparent cloak and flows,
But not upon my lips.

How can I sigh it? I fear it may
Mingle with earthly ether;
To whom shall I sing it? It dwells
In the house of my soul, in fear of
Harsh ears.

When I look into my inner eyes
I see the shadow of its shadow;
When I touch my fingertips
I feel its vibrations.
The deeds of my hands heed its
Presence as a lake must reflect
The glittering stars; my tears

Reveal it, as bright drops of dew
Reveal the secret of a withering rose.

It is a song composed by contemplation,
And published by silence,
And shunned by clamor,
And folded by truth,
And repeated by dreams,
And understood by love,
And hidden by awakening,
And sung by the soul.

It is the song of love;
What Cain or Esau could sing it?
It is more fragrant than jasmine;
What voice could enslave it?

It is heartbound, as a virgin's secret;
What strings could quiver it?
Who dares unite the roar of the sea
And the singing of the nightingale?
Who dares compare the shrieking tempest
To the sigh of an infant?
Who dares speak aloud the words
Intended for the heart to speak?
What human dares sing in voice
The song of God?

13

Laughter and Tears

As the Sun withdrew his rays from the garden, and the moon threw cushioned beams upon the flowers, I sat under the trees pondering upon the phenomena of the atmosphere, looking through the branches at the strewn stars which glittered like chips of silver upon a blue carpet; and I could hear from a distance the agitated murmur of the rivulet singing its way briskly into the valley.

When the birds took shelter among the boughs, and the flowers folded their petals, and tremendous silence descended, I heard a rustle of feet through the grass.

I took heed and saw a young couple approaching my arbor. They sat under a tree where I could see them without being seen.

After he looked about in every direction, I heard the young man saying, "Sit by me, my beloved, and listen to my heart; smile, for your happiness is a symbol of our future; be merry, for the sparkling days rejoice with us.

"My soul is warning me of the doubt in your heart, for doubt in love is a sin.

"Soon you will be the owner of this vast land, lighted by this beautiful moon; soon you will be the mistress of my palace, and all the servants and maids will obey your commands.

"Smile, my beloved, like the gold smiles from my father's coffers.

"My heart refuses to deny you its secret. Twelve months of comfort and travel await us; for a year we will spend my father's gold at the blue lakes of Switzerland, and viewing the edifices of Italy and Egypt, and resting under the Holy Cedars of Lebanon; you will meet the princesses who will envy you for your jewels and clothes.

"All these things I will do for you; will you be satisfied?"

In a little while I saw them walking and stepping on flowers as the rich step upon the hearts of the poor. As they disappeared from my sight, I commenced to make comparison between love and money, and to analyze their position in my heart.

Money! The source of insincere love; the spring of false light and fortune; the well of poisoned water; the desperation of old age!

I was still wandering in the vast desert of contemplation when a forlorn and specter-like couple passed by me and sat on the grass; a young man and a young woman who had left their farming shacks in the nearby fields for this cool and solitary place.

After a few moments of complete silence, I heard the following words uttered with sighs from weather-bitten lips, "Shed not tears, my beloved; love that opens our eyes and enslaves our hearts can give us the blessings of patience. Be consoled in our delay, for we have taken an oath and entered Love's shrine; for our love will ever grow in adversity; for it is in Love's name that we are suffering the obstacles of poverty and the sharpness of misery and the emptiness of separation. I shall attack these hardships until I triumph and place in your hands a strength that will help over all things to complete the journey of life.

Love—which is God—will consider our sighs and tears as incense burned at His altar and He will reward us with fortitude. Good-bye, my beloved; I must leave before the heartening moon vanishes."

A pure voice, combined of the consuming flame of love, and the hopeless bitterness of longing and the resolved sweetness of patience, said, "Good-bye, my beloved."

They separated, and the elegy to their union was smothered by the wails of my crying heart.

I looked upon slumbering Nature, and with deep reflection discovered the reality of a vast and infinite thing—something no power could demand, influence acquire, or riches purchase. Nor could it be effaced by the tears of time or deadened by sorrow; a thing which cannot be discovered by the blue lakes of Switzerland or the beautiful edifices of Italy.

It is something that gathers strength with patience, grows despite obstacles, warms in winter, flourishes in spring, casts a breeze in summer, and bears fruit in autumn—I found Love.

14

Song of the Flower

I am a kind word uttered and repeated
By the voice of Nature;
I am a star fallen from the
Blue tent upon the green carpet.
I am the daughter of the elements
With whom Winter conceived;
To whom Spring gave birth; I was
Reared in the lap of Summer and I
Slept in the bed of Autumn.

At dawn I unite with the breeze
To announce the coming of light;
At eventide I join the birds
In bidding the light farewell

The plains are decorated with
My beautiful colors, and the air
Is scented with my fragrance.

As I embrace Slumber the eyes of
Night watch over me, and as I

Awaken I stare at the sun, which is
The only eye of the day.

I drink dew for wine, and harken to
The voices of the birds, and dance
To the rhythmic swaying of the grass.

I am the lover's gift; I am the wedding wreath;
I am the memory of a moment of happiness;
I am the last gift of the living to the dead;
I am a part of joy and a part of sorrow.

But I look up high to see only the light,
And never look down to see my shadow.
This is wisdom which man must learn.

15

The Master and the Disciple

I. The Master's Journey to Venice

And it came to pass that the Disciple saw the Master walking silently to and fro in the garden, and signs of deep sorrow showed upon his pale face. The Disciple greeted the Master in the name of Allah, and inquired after the cause of his grief. The Master motioned with his staff, and bade the Disciple seat himself on the rock by the fish pond. The Disciple did so, and made ready to listen to the Master's story.

Said the Master:

"You desire me to tell you of the tragedy which Memory reenacts every day and night upon the stage of my heart. You are weary of my long silence and my unspoken secret, and you are troubled by my sighs and lamentations. To yourself you say, 'If the Master will not admit me into the temple of his sorrows, how shall I ever enter into the house of his affections?'

"Hearken to my story... Listen, but do not pity me; for pity is intended for the weak—and I am still strong in my affliction.

"From the days of my youth, I have been haunted, waking and sleeping, by the phantom of a strange woman. I see her when I am alone at night, sitting by my bedside. In the midnight silence I hear her heavenly voice. Often, when I close my eyes, I feel the touch of her gentle fingers upon my lips; and when I open my eyes, I am overcome with dread, and suddenly begin listening intently to the whispered sounds of Nothingness....

"Often I wonder, saying to myself, 'Is it my fancy that sets me spinning until I seem to lose myself in the clouds? Have I fashioned from the sinews of my dreams a new divinity with a melodious voice and a gentle touch? Have I lost my senses, and in my madness have I created this dearly loved companion? Have I withdrawn myself from the society of men and the clamor of the city so that I might be alone with the object of my adoration? Have I shut my eyes and ears to Life's forms and accents so that I might the better see her and hear her divine voice?'

"Often I wonder: 'Am I a madman who is content to be alone, and from the phantoms of his loneliness fashions a companion and spouse for his soul?'

"I speak of a *Spouse,* and you marvel at that word. But how often are we puzzled by some strange experience, which we reject as impossible, but whose reality we cannot efface from our minds, try as we will?

"This visionary woman has indeed been my spouse, sharing with me all the joys and sorrows of life. When I awake in the morning, I see her bending over my pillow, gazing at me with eyes glowing with kindness and maternal love. She is with me when I plan some undertaking, and she helps me bring it to fulfilment. When I sit down to my repast, she sits with me, and we exchange thoughts and words. In the evening, she is with me again, saying, 'We have tarried too long in this place. Let us walk in the fields and meadows.' Then I leave my work, and follow her into the fields, and we sit on a high rock and gaze at the distant horizon. She points to the golden cloud; and makes me aware of the song the birds sing before they retire for the night, thanking the Lord for the gift of freedom and peace.

"Many a time she comes to my room when I am anxious and troubled. But no sooner do I spy her, than all care and worry are turned to joy and calm. When my spirit rebels against man's injustice to man, and I see her face amidst those other faces I would flee from, the tempest in my heart subsides and is replaced by the heavenly voice of peace. When I am alone, and the bitter darts of life stab at my heart, and I am chained to the earth by life's shackles, I behold my companion gazing at me with love in her eyes, and sorrow turns to joy, and Life seems an Eden of happiness.

"You may ask, how can I be content with such a strange existence, and how can a man, like myself, in the springtime of life, find joy in phantoms and dreams? But I say to you, the years I have spent in this state am the cornerstone of all that I have come to know about Life, Beauty, Happiness, and Peace.

"For the companion of my imagination and I have been like thoughts freely hovering before the face of the sun, or floating on the surface of the waters, singing a song in the moonlight—a song of peace that soothes the spirit and leads it toward ineffable beauty.

"Life is that which we see and experience through the spirit; but the world around us we come to know through our understanding and reason. And such knowledge brings us great joy or sorrow. It was sorrow I was destined to experience before I reached the age of thirty. Would that I had died before I attained the years that drained my heart's blood and my life's sap, and left me a withered tree with branches that no longer move in the frolicsome breeze, and where birds no longer build their nests."

The Master paused, and then, seating himself by his Disciple, continued:

"Twenty years ago, the Governor of Mount Lebanon sent me to Venice on a scholarly mission, with a letter of recommendation to the Mayor of the city, whom he had met in Constantinople. I left Lebanon on an Italian vessel in the month of Nisan. The spring air was fragrant, and the white clouds hung above the horizon like so many lovely paintings. How shall I describe to you the exultation I felt during the journey? Words are too poor and too scant to express the inmost feeling in the heart of man.

"The years I spent with my ethereal companion were filled with contentment, joy, and peace. I never suspected that Pain lay in wait for me, or that Bitterness lurked at the bottom of my cup of Joy.

"As the carriage bore me away from my native hills and valleys, and toward the coast, my companion sat by my side. She was with me during the three joyful days I spent in Beirut, roaming the city with me, stopping where I stopped, smiling when a friend accosted me.

"When I sat on the balcony of the inn, overlooking the city, she joined me in my reveries.

"But when I was about to embark, a great change swept over me. I felt a strange hand seizing hold of me and pulling me back; and I heard a voice within me whispering, 'Turn back! Do not go! Turn back to the shore before the ship sets sail!'

"I did not heed that voice. But when the ship hoisted sail, I felt like a tiny bird that had suddenly been snatched between the claws of a hawk and was being borne aloft into the sky.

"In the evening, as the mountains and hills of Lebanon receded on the horizon, I found myself alone at the prow of the ship. I looked around for the woman of my dreams, the woman my heart loved, the spouse of my days, but she was no longer at my side. The beautiful maiden whose face I saw whenever I gazed at the sky, whose voice I heard in the stillness of the night, whose hand I held whenever I walked the streets of Beirut—was no longer with me.

"For the first time in my life I found myself utterly alone on a boat sailing the deep ocean. I paced the deck, calling to her in my heart, gazing on the waves in the hope of seeing her face. But all in vain. At midnight, when all the other passengers had retired, I remained on deck, alone, troubled, and anxious.

"Suddenly I looked up, and I saw her, the companion of my life, above me, in a cloud, a short distance from the prow. I leaped with joy, opened my arms wide, and cried out, 'Why have you forsaken me, my beloved! Where have you gone? Where have you been? Be near me now, and never leave me alone again!'

"She did not move. On her face I descried signs of sorrow and pain, something I had never seen before. Speaking softly and in sad tones she said, 'I have come from the depths of the ocean to see you once more. Now go down to your cabin, and give yourself over to sleep and dreams.'

"And having uttered these words, she became one with the clouds, and vanished. Like a hungry child I called to her frantically. I opened my arms in all directions, but all they embraced was the night air, heavy with dew.

"I went down to my berth, feeling within me the ebb and flow of the raging elements. It was as if I were on another boat altogether, being tossed on the rough seas of

Bewilderment and Despair.

"Strangely enough, as soon as I touched my pillow, I fell fast asleep.

"I dreamt, and in my dream I saw an apple tree shaped like a cross, and hanging from it, as if crucified, was the companion of my life. Drops of blood fell from her hands and feet upon the falling blossoms of the tree.

"The ship sailed on, day and night, but I was as though lost in a trance, not certain whether I was a human being sailing to a distant clime or a ghost moving across a cloudy sky. In vain I implored Providence for the sound of her voice, or a glimpse of her shadow, or the soft touch of her fingers on my lips.

"Fourteen days passed and I was still alone. On the fifteenth day, at noon, we sighted the coast of Italy at a distance, and at dusk we entered the harbor. A throng of people in gaily decorated gondolas came to greet the ship and convey the passengers to the city.

"The City of Venice is situated on many small islands, close to one another. Its streets are canals and its numerous palaces and residences are built on water. Gondolas are the only means of transportation.

"My gondolier asked where I was going, and when I told him to the Mayor of Venice, he looked at me with awe. As we moved through the canals, night was spreading her black cloak over the city. Lights gleamed from the open windows of palaces and churches, and their reflection in the water gave the city the appearance of something seen in a poet's dream, at once charming and enchanting.

"When the gondola reached the junction of two canals, I suddenly heard the mournful ringing of church bells. Though I was in a spiritual trance, and far removed from all reality, the sounds penetrated my heart and depressed my spirits.

"The gondola docked, and tied up at the foot of marble steps that led to a paved street. The gondolier pointed to a magnificent palace set in the middle of a garden and said: 'Here is your destination.' Slowly I climbed the steps leading to the palace, followed by the gondolier carrying my belongings. When I reached the gate, I paid him and dismissed him with my thanks.

"I rang, and the door was opened. As I entered I was greeted by sounds of wailing and weeping. I was startled and amazed. An elderly servant came toward me, and in a sorrowful voice asked what was my pleasure. 'Is this the palace of the Mayor?' I inquired. He bowed and nodded, and I handed him the missive given me by the Governor of Lebanon. He looked at it and solemnly walked toward the door leading to the reception room.

"I turned to a young servant and asked the cause of the sorrow that pervaded the room. He said that the Mayor's daughter had died that day, and as he spoke, he covered his face and wept bitterly.

"Imagine the feelings of a man who has crossed an ocean, all the while hovering between hope and despair, and at the end of his journey stands at the gate of a palace inhabited by the cruel phantoms of grief and lamentation. Imagine the feelings of a stranger seeking entertainment and hospitality in a palace, only to find himself welcomed by whitewinged Death.

"Soon the old servant returned, and bowing, said, 'The Mayor awaits you.'

"He led me to a door at the extreme end of a corridor, and motioned to me to enter. In the reception room I found a throng of priests and other dignitaries, all sunk in deep silence. In the center of the room, I was greeted by an elderly man with a long white beard, who shook my hand and said, 'It is our unhappy lot to welcome you, who come from a distant land, on a day that finds us bereft of our dearest daughter. Yet I trust our bereavement will not interfere with your mission, which, rest assured, I shall do all in my power to advance.'

"I thanked him for his kindness and expressed my deepest grief. Whereupon he led me to a seat, and I joined the rest of the silent throng.

"As I gazed at the sorrowful faces of the mourners, and listened to their painful sighs, I felt my heart contracting with grief and misery.

"Soon one after the other of the mourners took his departure, and only the grief-stricken father and I remained. When I, too, made a movement to leave, he held me back, and said, 'I beg you, my friend, do not go. Be our guest, if you can bear with us in our sorrow.'

"His words touched me deeply, and I bowed in acquiescence, and he continued, 'You men of Lebanon are most open-handed toward the stranger in your land. We should be seriously remiss in our duties were we to be less kind and courteous to our guest from Lebanon.' He rang, and in response to his summons a chamberlain appeared, attired in a magnificent uniform.

"'Show our guest to the room in the east wing,' he said, and take good care of him while he is with us.'

"The chamberlain conducted me to a spacious and lavishly appointed room. 'As soon as he was gone, I sank down on the couch, and began reflecting on my situation in this foreign land. I reviewed the first few hours I had spent here, so far away from the land of my birth.

"Within a few minutes, the chamberlain returned, bringing my supper on a silver tray. After I had eaten, I began pacing the room, stopping now and then at the window to look out upon the Venetian sky, and to listen to the shouts, of the gondoliers and the rhythmic beat of their oars. Before long I became drowsy, and dropping my wearied body on the bed, I gave myself over to an oblivion, in which was mingled the intoxication of sleep and the sobriety of wakefulness.

"I do not know how many hours I spent in this state, for there are vast spaces of life which the spirit traverses, and which we are unable to measure with time, the invention of man. All that I felt then, and feel now, is the wretched condition in which I found myself.

"Suddenly I became aware of a phantom hovering above me, of some ethereal spirit calling to me, but without any sensible signs. I stood up, and made my way toward the hall, as though prompted ants drawn by some divine force. I walked, will-less, as if in a dream, feeling as though I were journeying in a world that was beyond time and space.

"When I reached the end of the hall, I threw open a door and found myself in a vast chamber, in the center of which stood a coffin surrounded by flickering candles and wreaths of white flowers. I knelt by the side of the bier and looked upon the departed. There before me, veiled by death, was the face of my beloved, my life-long companion. It was the woman I worshipped, now cold in death, white-shrouded, surrounded by white flowers, and guarded by the silence of the ages.

"O Lord of Love, of Life, and of Death! Thou art the creator of our souls. Thou leanest our spirits toward light and darkness. Thou calmest our hearts and makest them to quicken with hope and pain. Now Thou hast shown me the companion of my youth in this cold and lifeless form.

"Lord, Thou hast plucked me from my land and hast

placed me in another, and revealed to me the power of Death over Life, and of Sorrow over Joy. Thou hast planted a white lily in the desert of my broken heart, and hast removed me to a distant valley to show me a withered one.

"Oh friends of my loneliness and exile: God has willed that I must drink the bitter cup of life. His will be done. We are naught but frail atoms in the heaven of the infinite; and we cannot but obey and surrender to the will of Providence.

"If we love, our love is neither from us, nor is it for us. If we rejoice, our joy is not in us, but in Life itself. If we suffer, our pain lies not in our wounds, but in the very heart of Nature.

"I do not complain, as I tell this tale; for he who complains doubts Life, and I am a firm believer. I believe in the worth of the bitterness mingled in each potion that I drink from the cup of Life. I believe in the beauty of the sorrow that penetrates my heart. I believe in the ultimate mercy of these steel fingers that crush my soul.

"This is my story. How can I end it, when in truth it has no ending?

"I remained on my knees before that coffin, lost in silence, and I stared at that angelic face until dawn came. Then I stood up and returned to my room, bowed under the heavy weight of Eternity, and sustained by the pain of suffering humanity.

"Three weeks later I left Venice and returned to Lebanon. It was as though I had spent aeons of years in the vast and silent depths of the past.

"But the vision remained. Though I had found her again only in death, in me she was still alive. In her shadow I have labored and learned. What those labors were, you, my disciple, know well.

"The knowledge and wisdom I have acquired I strove to bring to my people and their rulers. I brought to Al-Haris, Governor of Lebanon, the cry of the oppressed, who were being crushed under the injustices and evils of his State and Church officials.

"I counseled him to follow the path of his forefathers and to treat his subjects as they had done, with clemency, charity, and understanding. And I said to him, 'The people are the glory of our kingdom and the source of its wealth.' And I said further, 'There are four things a ruler should banish from his realm: Wrath, Avarice, Falsehood, and Violence.'

"For this and other teachings I was chastised, sent into exile, and excommunicated by the Church.

"There came a night when Al-Haris, troubled in heart, was unable to sleep. Standing at his window, he contemplated the firmament. Such marvels! So many heavenly bodies lost in the infinite! Who created this mysterious and admirable world? Who directs these stars in their courses? What relation have these distant planets to ours? Who am I and why am I here? All these things Al-Haris said to himself.

"Then he remembered my banishment and repented of the harsh treatment he had meted out to me. At once he sent for me, imploring my pardon. He honored me with an official robe and proclaimed me before all the people as his advisor, placing a golden key in my hand.

"For my years in exile I regret nothing. He who would seek Truth and proclaim it to mankind is bound to suffer. My sorrows have taught me to understand the sorrows of my fellow men; neither persecution nor exile have dimmed the vision within me.

"And now I am tired..."

Having finished his story, the Master dismissed his Disciple, whose name was Almuhtada, which means "the Convert," and went up to his retreat to rest body and soul from the fatigues of ancient memories.

II. The Death of the Master

Two weeks later, the Master fell ill, and a multitude of admirers came to the hermitage to inquire after his health. When they reached the gate of the garden, they saw coming out of the Master's quarters a priest, a nun, a doctor, and Almuhtada. The beloved Disciple announced the death of the Master. The crowd began to wail and lament, but Almuhtada neither wept nor spoke a word.

For a time the Disciple pondered within himself, then he stood upon the rock by the fish pond, and spoke:

"Brothers and countrymen: You have just heard the news of the Master's death. The immortal Prophet of Lebanon has given himself over to eternal sleep, and his blessed soul is hovering over us in the heavens of the spirit, high beyond all sorrow and mourning. His soul has cast off the servitude of the body and the fever and burdens of this earthly life.

"The Master has left this world of matter, attired in the garments of glory, and has gone to another world free of hardships and afflictions. He is now where our eyes cannot see him and our ears cannot hear him. He dwells in the world of the spirit, whose inhabitants sorely need him. He is now gathering knowledge in a new cosmos, whose history and beauty have always fascinated him and whose speech he has always striven to learn.

"His life on this earth was one long chain of great deeds. It was a life of constant thought; for the Master knew no rest except in work. He loved work, which he defined as *Visible Love.*

"His was a thirsty soul that could not rest except in the lap of wakefulness. His was a loving heart that overflowed with kindness and zeal.

"Such was the life he led on this earth....

"He was a spring of knowledge that issued from the bosom of Eternity, a pure stream of wisdom that waters and refreshes the mind of Man.

"And now that river has reached the shores of Eternal Life. Let no intruder lament for him or shed tears at his departure!

"Remember, only those who have stood before the Temple of Life, and never fructified the earth with one drop of the sweat of their brow are deserving your tears and lamentations when they leave it.

"But as for the Master—did he not spend all the days of his life laboring for the benefit of Mankind? Is there any among you who has not drunk from the pure fountain of his wisdom? And so, if you wish to honor him, offer his blessed soul a hymn of praise and thanksgiving, and not your mournful dirges and laments. If you wish to pay him due reverence, assert your claim to a portion of the knowledge in the books of wisdom he has left as a legacy to the world.

"Do not *give* to genius, but *take* from him! Thus only shall you be honoring him. Do not mourn for him, but be merry, and drink deeply of his wisdom. Only thus will you be paying him the tribute rightly his."

After hearing the words of the Disciple, the multitude returned to their homes, with smiles upon their lips, and songs of thanksgiving in their hearts.

Almuhtada was left alone in this world; but loneliness never possessed his heart, for the voice of the Master always resounded in his ears, urging him to carry on his work and sow the words of the Prophet in the hearts and minds of all who would listen of their own free will. He spent many hours alone in the garden meditating upon the scrolls which the Master had bequeathed to him, and in which he had set down his words of wisdom.

After forty days of meditation, Almuhtada left his Master's retreat and began his wanderings through the hamlets, villages, and cities of Ancient Phoenicia.

One day, as he was crossing the market place of the city of Beirut, a multitude followed him. He stopped at a public walk, and the throng gathered around him, and he spoke to them with the voice of the Master, saying:

"The tree of my heart is heavy with fruit; come, ye hungry ones, and gather it. Eat and be satisfied.... Come and receive from the bounty of my heart and lighten my burden. My soul is weary under the weight of gold and silver. Come, ye seekers after hidden treasures, fill your purses and relieve me of my burden....

"My heart overflows with the wine of the ages. Come, all ye thirsty ones, drink and quench your thirst.

"The other day I saw a rich man standing at the temple door, stretching out his hands, which were full of precious stones, toward all passers-by, and calling to them, saying; 'Have pity on me. Take these jewels from me. For they have made my soul sick and hardened my heart. Pity me, take them, and make me whole again.'

"But none of the passers-by paid heed to his pleas.

"And I looked at the man, and I said to myself, 'Surely it were better for him to be a pauper, roaming the streets of Beirut, stretching out a trembling hand for alms, and returning home at eventide empty-handed.'

"I have seen a wealthy and open-handed sheik of Damascus, pitching his tents in the wilderness of the Arabian desert, and by the sides of the mountains. In the evening he sent his slaves out to waylay travelers and bring them to his tents to be sheltered and entertained. But the rough roads were deserted, and the servants brought him no guests.

"And I pondered the plight of the lonely sheik, and my heart spoke to me, saying: 'Surely it is better for him to be a straggler, with a staff in his hand and an empty bucket hanging from his arm, sharing at noontide the bread of friendship with his companions by the refuse heaps at the edge of the city....'

"In Lebanon I saw the Governor's daughter rising from her slumber, attired in a precious gown. Her hair was sprinkled with musk and her body was anointed with perfume. She walked into the garden of her father's palace, seeking a lover. The dewdrops upon the carpeted grass moistened the hem of her garment. But alas! Among all her father's subjects there was no one who loved her.

"As I meditated upon the wretched state of the Governor's daughter, my soul admonished me, saying, 'Were it not better for her to be the daughter of a simple peasant, leading her father's flocks to pasture and bringing them back to the fold in the evening, with the fragrance of the earth and of the vineyards in her coarse shepherd's gown? At the very least, she could steal away from her father's hut, and in the silence of the night walk toward her beloved, waiting for her by the murmuring brook!'

"The tree of my heart is heavy with fruit. Come, ye

hungry souls, gather it, eat and be satisfied. My spirit overflows with aged wine. Come, oh ye thirsty hearts, drink and quench your thirst....

"Would that I were a tree that neither blossoms nor bears fruit; for the pain of fertility is harsher than the bitterness of barrenness; and the ache of the open-handed rich is more terrible than the misery of the wretched poor....

"Would that I were a dry well, so people might throw stones into my depths. For it is better to be an empty well than a spring of pure water untouched by thirsty lips.

"Would I were a broken reed, trampled by the foot of man, for that is better than to be a lyre in the house of one whose fingers are blistered and whose household is deaf to sound.

"Hear me, Oh ye sons and daughters of my motherland; meditate upon these words that come to you through the voice of the Prophet. Make room for them in the precincts of your heart, and let wisdom's seed blossom in the garden of your soul. For that is the precious gift of the Lord."

❧

And the fame of Almuhtada spread all over the land, and many people came to him from other countries to do him reverence and to listen to the spokesman of the Master.

Physicians, men-of-law, poets, philosophers overwhelmed him with questions whenever they would meet him, whether in the street, in the church, in the mosque, or in the synagogue, or any other place where men foregather. Their minds were enriched by his beautiful words, which passed from lips to lips.

He spoke to them of Life and the Reality of Life, saying:

"Man is like the foam of the sea, that floats upon the surface of the water. When the wind blows, it vanishes, as if it had never been. Thus are our lives blown away by Death....

"The Reality of Life is Life itself, whose beginning is not in the womb, and whose ending is not in the grave. For the years that pass are naught but a moment in eternal life; and the world of matter and all in it is but a dream compared to the awakening which we call the terror of Death.

"The ether carries every sound of laughter, every sigh that comes from our hearts, and preserves their echo, which responds to every kiss whose source is joy.

"The angels keep count of every tear shed by Sorrow; and they bring to the ears of the spirits hovering in the heavens of the Infinite each song of Joy wrought from our affections.

"There, in the world to come, we shall see and feel all the vibrations of our feelings and the motions of our hearts. We shall understand the meaning of the divinity within us, whom we condemn because we are prompted by Despair.

"That deed which in our guilt we today call weakness, will appear tomorrow as an essential link in the complete chain of Man.

"The cruel tasks for which we received no reward will live with us, and show forth in splendor, and declare our glory; and the hardships we have sustained shall be as a wreath of laurel on our honored heads..."

Having uttered these words, the Disciple was about to withdraw from the crowds and repose his body from the labors of the day, when he spied a young man gazing at a lovely girl, with eyes that reflected bewilderment.

And the Disciple addressed him, saying:

"Are you troubled by the many faiths that Mankind

professes? Are you lost in the valley of conflicting beliefs? Do you think that the freedom of heresy is less burdensome than the yoke of submission, and the liberty of dissent safer than the stronghold of acquiescence?

"If such be the case, then make Beauty your religion, and worship her as your godhead; for she is the visible, manifest and perfect handiwork of God. Cast off those who have toyed with godliness as if it were a sham, joining together greed and arrogance; but believe instead in the divinity of beauty that is at once the beginning of your worship of Life, and the source of your hunger for Happiness.

"Do penance before Beauty, and atone for your sins, for Beauty brings your heart closer to the throne of woman, who is the mirror of your affections and the teacher of your heart in the ways of Nature, which is your life's home."

And before dismissing the assembled throng, he added:

"In this world there are two sorts of men: the men of yesterday and the men of tomorrow. To which of these do you belong, my brethren? Come, let me gaze at you, and learn whether you are of those entering into the world of light, or of those going forth into the land of darkness. Come, tell me who you are and what you are.

"Are you a politician who says to himself: 'I will use my country for my own benefit'? If so, you are naught but a parasite living on the flesh of others. Or are you a devoted patriot, who whispers into the ear of his inner self: 'I love to serve my country as a faithful servant.' If so, you are an oasis in the desert, ready to quench the thirst of the wayfarer.

"Or are you a merchant, drawing advantage from the needs of the people, engrossing goods so as to resell them at an exorbitant price? If so, you are a reprobate; and it matters naught whether your home is a palace or a prison.

"Or are you an honest man, who enables farmer and weaver to exchange their products, who mediates between buyer and seller, and through his just ways profits both himself and others?

"If so, you are a righteous man; and it matters not whether you are praised or blamed.

"Are you a leader of religion, who weaves out of the simplicity of the faithful a scarlet robe for his body; and of their kindness a golden crown for his head; and while living on Satan's plenty, spews forth his hatred of Satan? If so, you are a heretic; and it matters not that you fast all day and pray all night.

"Or are you the faithful one who finds in the goodness of people a groundwork for the betterment of the whole nation; and in whose soul is the ladder of perfection leading to the Holy Spirit? If you are such, you are like a lily in the garden of Truth; and it matters not if your fragrance is lost upon men, or dispersed into the air, where it will be eternally preserved.

"Or are you a journalist who sells his principles in the markets of slaves and who fattens on gossip and misfortune and crime? If so, you are like a ravenous vulture preying upon rotting carrion.

"Or are you a teacher standing upon the raised stage of history, who, inspired by the glories of the past, preaches to mankind and acts as he preaches? If so, you are a restorative to ailing humanity and a balm for the wounded heart.

"Are you a governor looking down on those you govern, never stirring abroad except to rifle their pockets or to exploit them for your own profit? If so, you are like tares upon the threshing floor of the nation.

"Are you a devoted servant who loves the people and is

ever watchful over their welfare, and zealous for their success? If so, you are as a blessing in the granaries of the land.

"Or are you a husband who regards the wrongs he has committed as lawful, but those of his wife as unlawful? If so, you are like those extinct savages who lived in caves and covered their nakedness with hides.

"Or are you a faithful companion, whose wife is ever at his side, sharing his every thought, rapture, and victory? If so, you are as one who at dawn walks at the head of a nation toward the high noon of justice, reason and wisdom.

"Are you a writer who holds his head high above the crowd, while his brain is deep in the abyss of the past, that is filled with the tatters and useless cast-offs of the ages? If so, you are like a stagnant pool of water.

"Or are you the keen thinker, who scrutinizes his inner self, discarding that which is useless, outworn and evil, but preserving that which is useful and good? If so, you are as manna to the hungry, and as cool, clear water to the thirsty.

"Are you a poet full of noise and empty sounds? If so, you are like one of those mountebanks that make us laugh when they are weeping, and make us weep, when they laugh.

"Or are you one of those gifted souls in whose hands God has placed a viol to soothe the spirit with heavenly music, and bring his fellow men close to Life and the Beauty of Life? If so, you are a torch to light us on our way, a sweet longing in our hearts, and a revelation of the divine in our dreams.

"Thus is mankind divided into two long columns, one composed of the aged and bent, who support themselves on crooked staves, and as they walk on the path of Life, they pant as if they were climbing toward a mountaintop, while they are actually descending into the abyss.

"And the second column is composed of youth, running as with winged feet, singing as if their throats were strung with silver strings, and climbing toward the mountaintop as though drawn by some irresistible, magic power.

"In which of these two processions do you belong, my brethren? Ask yourselves this question, when you are alone in the silence of the night.

"Judge for yourselves whether you belong with the Slaves of Yesterday or the Free Men of Tomorrow."

And Almuhtada returned to his retreat, and kept himself in seclusion for many months, while he read and pondered the words of wisdom the Master had set down in the scrolls bequeathed to him. He learned much; but there were many things he found he had not learned, nor ever heard from the lips of the Master. He vowed that he would not leave the hermitage until he had thoroughly studied and mastered all that the Master had left behind, so that he might deliver it to his countrymen. In this way Almuhtada became engrossed in the perusal of his Master's words, oblivious of himself and all around him, and forgetting all those who had hearkened to him in the market places and streets of Beirut.

In vain his admirers tried to reach him, having become concerned about him. Even when the Governor of Mount Lebanon summoned him with a request that he address the officials of the state, he declined, saying, "I shall come back to you soon, with a special message for all the people."

The Governor decreed that on the day Almuhtada was to appear all citizens should receive and welcome him with honor in their homes, and in the churches, mosques, synagogues, and houses of learning, and they should hearken with reverence to his words, for his was the voice of the Prophet.

The day when Almuhtada finally emerged from his retreat to begin his mission became a day of rejoicing and festivity for all. Almuhtada spoke freely and without hindrance; he preached the gospel of love and brotherhood. No one dared threaten him with exile from the country or excommunication from the Church. How unlike the fate of his Master, whose portion had been banishment and excommunication, before eventual pardon and recall!

Almuhtada's words were heard all over Lebanon. Later they were printed in a book, in the form of epistles, and distributed in Ancient Phoenicia and other Arabic lands. Some of the epistles are in the Master's own words; others were culled by Master and Disciple from ancient books of wisdom and lore.

16

A Poet's Voice

Part One

The power of charity sows deep in my heart, and I reap and gather the wheat in bundles and give them to the hungry.

My soul gives life to the grapevine and I press its bunches and give the juice to the thirsty.

Heaven fills my lamp with oil and I place it at my window to direct the stranger through the dark.

I do all these things because I live in them; and if destiny should tie my hands and prevent me from so doing, then death would be my only desire. For I am a poet, and if I cannot give, I shall refuse to receive.

Humanity rages like a tempest, but I sigh in silence for I know the storm must pass away while a sigh goes to God.

Human kinds cling to earthly things, but I seek ever to embrace the torch of love so it will purify me by its fire and sear inhumanity from my heart.

Substantial things deaden a man without suffering; love awakens him with enlivening pains.

Humans are divided into different clans and tribes,

and belong to countries and towns. But I find myself a stranger to all communities and belong to no settlement. The universe is my country and the human family is my tribe.

Men are weak, and it is sad that they divide amongst themselves. The world is narrow and it is unwise to cleave it into kingdoms, empires, and provinces.

Human kinds unite themselves only to destroy the temples of soul, and they join hands to build edifices for earthly bodies. I stand alone listening to the voice of hope in my deep self saying, "As love enlivens a man's heart with pain, so ignorance teaches him the way to knowledge." Pain and ignorance lead to great joy and knowledge because the Supreme Being has created nothing vain under the sun.

Part Two

I have a yearning for my beautiful country, and I love its people because of their misery. But if my people rose, stimulated by plunder and motivated by what they call "patriotic spirit" to murder, and invaded my neighbour's country, then upon the committing of any human atrocity I would hate my people and my country.

I sing the praise of my birthplace and long to see the home of my childhood; but if the people in that home refused to shelter and feed the needy wayfarer, I would convert my praise into anger and my longing into forgetfulness. My inner voice would say, "The house that does not comfort the needy is worthy of naught but destruction."

I love my native village with some of my love for my country; and I love my country with part of my love for the earth, all of which is my country; and I love the earth with all of myself because it is the haven of humanity, the manifest spirit of God.

Humanity is the spirit of the Supreme Being on earth, and that humanity is standing amidst ruins, hiding its nakedness behind tattered rags, shedding tears upon hollow cheeks, and calling for its children with pitiful voice. But the children are busy singing their clan's anthem; they are busy sharpening the swords and cannot hear the cry of their mothers.

Humanity appeals to its people but they listen not. Were one to listen, and console a mother by wiping her tears, others would say, "He is weak, affected by sentiment."

Humanity is the spirit of the Supreme Being on earth, and that Supreme Being preaches love and good-will. But the people ridicule such teachings. The Nazarene Jesus listened, and crucifixion was his lot; Socrates heard the voice and followed it, and he too fell victim in body. The followers of The Nazarene and Socrates are the followers of Deity, and since people will not kill them, they deride them, saying, "Ridicule is more bitter than killing."

Jerusalem could not kill The Nazarene, nor Athens Socrates; they are living yet and shall live eternally. Ridicule cannot triumph over the followers of Deity. They live and grow forever.

Part Three

Thou art my brother because you are a human, and we both are sons of one Holy Spirit; we are equal and made of the same earth.

You are here as my companion along the path of life, and my aid in understanding the meaning of hidden Truth. You are a human, and, that fact sufficing, I love you as a brother. You may speak of me as you choose, for Tomorrow shall take you away and will use your talk as evidence for his judgment, and you shall receive justice.

You may deprive me of whatever I possess, for my greed instigated the amassing of wealth and you are entitled to my lot if it will satisfy you.

You may do unto me whatever you wish, but you shall not be able to touch my Truth.

You may shed my blood and burn my body, but you cannot kill or hurt my spirit.

You may tie my hands with chains and my feet with shackles, and put me in the dark prison, but you shall not enslave my thinking, for it is free, like the breeze in the spacious sky.

You are my brother and I love you. I love you worshipping in your church, kneeling in your temple, and praying in your mosque. You and I and all are children of one religion, for the varied paths of religion are but the fingers of the loving hand of the Supreme Being, extended to all, offering completeness of spirit to all, anxious to receive all.

I love you for your Truth, derived from your knowledge; that Truth which I cannot see because of my ignorance. But I respect it as a divine thing, for it is the deed of the spirit, Your Truth shall meet my Truth in the coming world and blend together like the fragrance of flowers and become one whole and eternal Truth, perpetuating and living in the eternity of Love and Beauty.

I love you because you are weak before the strong oppressor, and poor before the greedy rich. For these reasons I shed tears and comfort you; and from behind my tears I see you embraced in the arms of Justice, smiling and forgiving your persecutors. You are my brother and I love you.

Part Four

You are my brother, but why are you quarreling with me? Why do you invade my country and try to subjugate me for the sake of pleasing those who are seeking glory and authority?

Why do you leave your wife and children and follow Death to the distant land for the sake of those who buy glory with your blood, and high honour with your mother's tears?

Is it an honour for a man to kill his brother man? If you deem it an honour, let it be an act of worship, and erect a temple to Cain who slew his brother Abel.

Is self-preservation the first law of Nature? Why, then, does Greed urge you to self-sacrifice in order only to achieve his aim in hurting your brothers? Beware, my brother, of the leader who says, "Love of existence obliges us to deprive the people of their rights!" I say unto you but this: protecting others' rights is the noblest and most beautiful human act; if my existence requires that I kill others, then death is more honourable to me, and if I cannot find someone to kill me for the protection of my honour, I will not hesitate to take my life by my own hands for the sake of Eternity before Eternity comes.

Selfishness, my brother, is the cause of blind superiority, and superiority creates clanship, and clanship creates authority which leads to discord and subjugation.

The soul believes in the power of knowledge and justice over dark ignorance; it denies the authority that supplies the swords to defend and strengthen ignorance and oppression—that authority which destroyed Babylon and shook the foundation of Jerusalem and left Rome in ruins. It is that which made people call criminals great men; made writers respect their names; made historians relate the stories of their inhumanity in manner of praise.

The only authority I obey is the knowledge of guarding and acquiescing in the Natural Law of Justice.

What justice does authority display when it kills the killer? When it imprisons the robber? When it descends on a neighbouring country and slays its people? What does justice think of the authority under which a killer punishes the one who kills, and a thief sentences the one who steals?

You are my brother, and I love you; and Love is justice with its full intensity and dignity. If justice did not support my love for you, regardless of your tribe and community, I would be a deceiver concealing the ugliness of selfishness behind the outer garment of pure love.

Conclusion

My soul is my friend who consoles me in misery and distress of life. He who does not befriend his soul is an enemy of humanity, and he who does not find human guidance within himself will perish desperately. Life emerges from within, and derives not from environs.

I came to say a word and I shall say it now. But if death prevents its uttering, it will be said by Tomorrow, for Tomorrow never leaves a secret in the book of Eternity.

I came to live in the glory of Love and the light of Beauty, which are the reflections of God. I am here living, and the people are unable to exile me from the domain of life for they know I will live in death. If they pluck my eyes I will hearken to the murmurs of Love and the songs of Beauty.

If they close my ears I will enjoy the touch of the breeze mixed with the incense of Love and the fragrance of Beauty.

If they place me in vacuum, I will live together with my soul, the child of Love and Beauty.

I came here to be for all and with all, and what I do today in my solitude will be echoed by Tomorrow to the people.

What I say now with one heart will be said tomorrow by many hearts.

17

The Poet From Baalbek

Sarkis Effandi, one of Gibran's closest friends, was highly regarded among the intelligentsia of Lebanon. He owned a publishing house and a daily Arabic newspaper called Lisan-Ul-Hal. In the year 1912, the Arab League of Progress, organized for the promotion of Arab unity and culture, decided to honor the great Lebanese poet Khalil Effandi Mutran.

Since Sarkis was the head of the committee honoring the poet, he extended an invitation to his friend Gibran, now settled in New York, to join them in Beirut on that occasion. Gibran could not make the trip, but he sent Sarkis a story with instructions to read it in his behalf before the poet. In the story, which eulogises the poet, Gibran expresses his belief in the transmigration of souls and praises the great soul reincarnated in the honored poet.

In the City of Baalbek, the Year 112 B.C.

The Emir sat on his golden throne surrounded by glittering lamps and gilded censers. The aromatic scent of the latter filled the palace. At his right and left sides were the high priests and the chiefs; the slaves and guards stood immobile before him like statues of bronze erected before the face of the sun.

After the cantors had chanted echoing hymns, an elderly vizier stood before the Emir, and in a voice modulated in the serenity of age, said, "Oh great and merciful Prince, yesterday there arrived in our city a sage from India who believes in a diversity of religions and speaks of strange things difficult to understand. He preaches the doctrine of the transmigration of souls and the incarnation of spirits which move from one generation to another seeking more and more perfect avatars until they become godlike. This sage seeks an audience with you to explain his dogma."

The Emir shook his bead, smiled, and said, "From India come many strange and wonderful things. Call in the sage that we may hear his words of wisdom."

As soon as he uttered these words, a dark-hued, aged man walked in with dignity and stood before the Emir. His large brown eyes spoke, without words, of deep secrets. He bowed, raised his head, his eyes glittered, and be commenced to speak.

He explained how the spirits pass from one body to another, elevated by the good acts of the medium which they choose, and influenced by their experience in each existence; aspiring toward a splendor that exalts them and strengthens their growth by Love that makes them both happy and miserable....

Then the philosopher dwelt on the manner in which the spirits move from place to place in their quest for perfection, atoning in the present for sins committed in the past, and reaping in one existence what they had sown in another.

Observing signs of restlessness and weariness on the Emir's countenance, the old vizier whispered to the sage, "You have preached enough at present; please postpone the rest of your discourse until our next meeting."

Thereupon the sage withdrew from the Emir's presence and sat among the priests and chiefs, closing his eyes as if weary of gazing into the deeps of Existence.

After a profound silence, similar to the trance of a prophet, the Emir looked to the right and to the left and inquired, "Where is our poet, we have not seen him for many days. What became of him? He always attended our meeting."

A priest responded, saying, "A week ago I saw him sitting in the portico of Ishtar's temple, staring with glazed and sorrowful eyes at the distant evening twilight as if one of his poems had strayed among the clouds."

And a chief added, "I saw him yesterday standing beneath the shade of the willow and cypress trees. I greeted him but be gave no heed to my greeting, and remained submerged in the deep sea of his thoughts and meditations."

Then the Grand Eunuch said, "I saw him today in the palace garden, with pale and haggard face, sighing, and his eyes full of tears."

"Go seek out this unhappy soul, for his absence from our midst troubles us," ordered the Emir.

At this command, the slaves and the guards left the hall to seek the poet, while the Emir and his priests and chiefs remained in the assembly hall awaiting their return. It seemed as if their spirits had felt his invisible presence among them.

Soon the Grand Eunuch returned and prostrated himself at the feet of the Emir like a bird shot by the arrow of an archer. Whereupon the Emir shouted at him saying, "What happened... what have you to say?" The slave raised his head and said in a trembling voice, "We found the poet dead in the palace garden."

Then the Emir rose and hastened sorrowfully to the palace garden, preceded by his torchbearers and followed by the priests and the chiefs. At the end of the garden close by the almond and pomegranate trees, the yellow light of the torches brought the dead youth into their sight. His corpse lay upon the green grass like a withered rose.

"Look how he embraced his viol as if the two were lovers pledged to die together!" said one of the Emir's aides.

Another one said, "He still stares, as in life, at the heart of space; he still seems to be watching the invisible movements of an unknown god among the planets."

And the high priest addressed the Emir, saying, "Tomorrow let us bury him, as a great poet, in the shade of Ishtar's temple, and let the townspeople march in his funeral procession, while youths sing his poems and virgins strew flowers over his sepulchre. Let it be a commemoration worthy of his genius."

The Emir nodded his head without diverting his eyes from the young poet's face, pale with the veil of Death. "We have neglected this pure soul when he was alive, filling the Universe with the fruit of his brilliant intellect and spreading throughout space the aromatic scent of his soul. If we do not honor him now, we will be mocked and reviled by the gods and the nymphs of the prairies and valleys.

"Bury him in this spot where he breathed his last and let his viol remain between his arms. If you wish to honor him and pay him tribute, tell your children that the Emir had neglected him and was the cause of his miserable and lonely death." Then the monarch asked, "Where is the sage from India?" And the sage walked forth and said, "Here, oh great Prince."

And the Emir inquired, saying, "Tell us, oh sage, will the gods ever restore me to this world as a prince and bring back the deceased poet to life? Will my spirit become incarnated in a body of a great king's son, and will the poet's soul transmigrate into the body of another genius? Will the sacred Law make him stand before the face of Eternity that he may compose poems of Life? Will he be restored that I may honor him and pay him tribute by showering upon him precious gifts and rewards that will enliven his heart and inspire his soul?"

And the sage answered the Emir, saying, "*Whatever the soul longs for, will be attained by the spirit.* Remember, oh great Prince, that the sacred Law which restores the sublimity of Spring after the passing of Winter will reinstate you a prince and him a genius poet."

The Emir's hopes were revived and signs of joy appeared on his face. He walked toward his palace thinking and meditating upon the words of the sage: "*Whatever the soul longs for, wilt be attained by the spirit.*"

In Cairo, Egypt, the Year 1912 A.D.

The full moon appeared and spread her silver garment upon the city. The Prince of the land stood at the balcony of his palace gazing at the clear sky and pondering upon the ages that have passed along the bank of the Nile. He seemed to be reviewing the processions of the nations that marched, together with Time, from the Pyramid to the palace of Abedine.

As the circle of the Prince's thoughts widened and extended into the domain of his dreams, he looked at his boon companion sitting by his side and said, "My soul is thirsty; recite a poem for me tonight."

And the boon companion bowed his head and began a

pre-Islamic poem. But before he had recited many stanzas, the Prince interrupted him saying, "Let us hear a modern poem... a more recent one."

And, bowing, the boon companion began to recite verses composed by a Hadramout poet. The Prince stopped him again, saying, "More recent... a more recent poem."

The singer raised his hand and touched his forehead as if trying to recall to memory all the poems composed by contemporary poets. Then his eyes glittered, his face brightened, and he began to sing lovely verses in soothing rhythm, full of enchantment.

Intoxicated and seeming to feel the movement of hidden hands beckoning him from his palace to a distant land, the Prince fervently inquired, "Who composed these verses?" And the singer answered, "The Poet from Baalbek."

The Poet from Baalbek is an ancient name and it brought into the Prince's memory images of forgotten days. It awakened in the depth of his heart phantoms of remembrance, and drew before his eyes, with lines formed by the mist, a picture of a dead youth embracing his viol and surrounded by priests, chiefs, and ministers.

Like dreams dissipated by the light of Morn, the vision soon left the Prince's eyes. He stood up and walked toward his palace with crossed arms repeating the words of Mohammed, *"You were dead and He brought you back to life, and He will return you to the dead and then restore you to life. Whereupon you shall go back to Him."*

Then he looked at his boon companion and said, "We are fortunate to have the Poet from Baalbek in our land, and shall make it our paramount duty to honor and befriend him." After a few moments worthy of silence and respect, the Prince added in a low voice, "The poet is a bird of strange moods. He descends from his lofty domain to tarry among us, singing; if we do not honor him he will unfold his wings and fly back to his dwelling place."

The night was over, and the skies doffed their garments studded with stars, and put on raiment woven from the sinews of the rays of Morn. And the Prince's soul swayed between the wonders and strangeness of Existence and the concealed mysteries of Life.

18

Union

When the night had embellished heaven's garment with the stars' gems, there rose a houri from the Valley of the Nile and hovered in the sky on invisible wings. She sat upon a throne of mist hung between heaven and the sea. Before her passed a host of angels chanting in unison, "Holy, holy, holy the daughter of Egypt whose grandeur fills the globe."

Then on the summit of Fam el Mizab, girdled by the forest of the cedars, a phantom youth was raised by the hands of the seraphim, and he sat upon the throne beside the houri. The spirits circled them singing, "Holy, holy, holy the youth of Lebanon, whose magnificence fills the ages."

And when the suitor held the hands of his beloved and gazed into her eyes, the wave and wind carried their communion to all the universe:

How faultless is your radiance, Oh daughter of Isis, and how great my adoration for you!

How graceful you are among the youths, Oh son of Astarte, and how great my yearning for you!

My love is as strong as your Pyramids, and the ages shall not destroy it.

My love is as staunch as your Holy Cedars, and the

elements shall not prevail over it.

The wise men of all the nations come from East and West to discern your wisdom and to interpret your signs.

The scholars of the world come from all the kingdoms to intoxicate themselves with the nectar of your beauty and the magic of your voice.

Your palms are fountains of abundance.

Your arms are springs of pure water, and your breath is a refreshing breeze.

The palaces and temples of the Nile announce your glory, and the Sphinx narrates your greatness.

The cedars upon your bosom are like a medal of honor, and the towers about you speak your bravery and might.

Oh how sweet is your love and how wonderful is the hope that you foster.

Oh what a generous partner you are, and how faithful a spouse you have proved to be. How sublime are your gifts, and how precious your sacrifice!

You sent to me young men who were as an awakening after deep slumber. You gave me men of daring to conquer the weakness of my people, and scholars to exalt them, and geniuses to enrich their powers.

From the seeds I sent you you wrought flowers; from saplings you raised trees. For you are a virgin meadow on which roses and lilies grow and the cypresses and the cedar trees rise.

I see sorrow in your eyes, my beloved; do you grieve while you are at my side?

I have sons and daughters who emigrated beyond the seas and left me weeping and longing for their return.

Are you afraid, oh daughter of the Nile, and dearest of all nations?

I fear a tyrant approaching me with a sweet voice so that he may later rule me with the strength of his arms.

The life of the nations, my love, is like the life of individuals; a life cheered by Hope and married to Fear, beset by desires and frowned upon by Despair.

And the lovers embraced and kissed and drank from the cups of love the scented wine of the ages; and the host of spirits chanted, "Holy, holy, holy, Love's glory fills heaven and earth."

19

My Soul Preached to Me

My soul preached to me and taught me to love that which the people abhor and befriend him whom they revile.

My soul showed me that Love prides itself not only in the one who loves, but also in the beloved.

Ere my soul preached to me, Love was in my heart as a tiny thread fastened between two pegs.

But now Love has become a halo whose beginning is its end, and whose end is its beginning. It surrounds every being and extends slowly to embrace all that shall be.

❧

My soul advised me and taught me to perceive the hidden beauty of the skin, figure, and hue. She instructed me to meditate upon that which the people call ugly until its true charm and delight appear.

Ere my soul counselled me, I saw Beauty like a trembling torch between columns of smoke. Now since the smoke has vanished, I see naught save the flame.

My soul preached to me and taught me to listen to the voices which the tongue and the larynx and the lips do not utter.

Ere my soul preached to me, I heard naught but

clamor and wailing. But now I eagerly attend Silence and hear its choirs singing the hymns of the ages and the songs of the firmament announcing the secrets of the Unseen.

❧

My soul preached to me and instructed me to drink the wine that cannot be pressed and cannot be poured from cups that hands can lift or lips can touch.

Ere my soul preached to me, my thirst was like a dim spark hidden under the ashes that can be extinguished by a swallow of water.

But now my longing has become my cup, my affections my wine, and my loneliness my intoxication; yet, in this unquenchable thirst there is eternal joy.

My soul preached to me and taught me to touch that which has not become incarnate; my soul revealed to me that whatever we touch is part of our desire.

But now my fingers have turned into mist penetrating that which is seen in the universe and mingling with the Unseen.

My soul instructed me to inhale the scent that no myrtle or incense emits. Ere my soul preached to me, I craved the scent of perfume in the gardens or in flasks or in censers.

But now I can savor the incense that is not burnt for offering or sacrifice. And I fill my heart with a fragrance that has never been wafted by the frolicsome breeze of space.

My soul preached to me and taught me to say, "I am ready" when the Unknown and Danger call on me.

Ere my soul preached to me, I answered no voice save the voice of the crier whom I knew, and walked not save upon the easy and smooth path.

Now the Unknown has become a steed that I can mount in order to reach the Unknown; and the plain has turned into a ladder on whose steps I climb to the summit.

My soul spoke to me and said, "Do not measure Time by saying, 'There was yesterday, and there shall be tomorrow.'"

And ere my soul spoke to me, I imagined the Past as an epoch that never returned, and the Future as one that could never be reached.

Now I realize that the present moment contains all time and within it is all that can be hoped for, done and realized.

My soul preached to me exhorting me not to limit space by saying, "Here, there, and yonder."

Ere my soul preached to me, I felt that wherever I walked was far from any other space.

Now I realize that wherever I am contains all places; and the distance that I walk embraces all distances.

My soul instructed me and advised me to stay awake while others sleep. And to surrender to slumber when others are astir.

Ere my soul preached to me, I saw not their dreams in my sleep, neither did they observe my vision.

Now I never sail the vessel of my dreams unless they watch me, and they never soar into the sky of their vision unless I rejoice in their freedom.

❧

My soul preached to me and said, "Do not be delighted because of praise, and do not be distressed because of blame."

Ere my soul counselled me, I doubted the worth of my work.

Now I realize that the trees blossom in Spring and bear fruit in Summer without seeking praise; and they drop their leaves in Autumn and become naked in Winter without fearing blame.

My soul preached to me and showed me that I am neither more than the pygmy, nor less than the giant.

Ere my soul preached to me, I looked upon humanity as two men: one weak, whom I pitied, and the other strong, whom I followed or resisted in defiance.

But now I have learned that I was as both are and made from the same elements. My origin is their origin, my conscience is their conscience, my contention is their contention, and my pilgrimage is their pilgrimage.

If they sin, I am also a sinner. If they do well, I take pride in their well-doing. If they rise, I rise with them. If they stay inert, I share their slothfulness.

❧

My soul spoke to me and said, "The lantern which you carry is not yours, and the song that you sing was not composed within your heart, for even if you bear the light, you are not the light, and even if you are a lute fastened with strings, you are not the lute player."

❧

My soul preached to me, my brother, and taught me much. And your soul has preached and taught as much to you. For you and I are one, and there is no variance between us save that I urgently declare that which is in my inner self, while you keep as a secret that which is within you. But in your secrecy there is a sort of virtue.

20

Vision

When Night came and Slumber spread its garment upon the face of the earth, I left my bed and walked toward the sea saying, "The sea never sleeps, and in its vigil there is consolation for a sleepless soul."

When I reached the shore, the mist from the mountains had engauzed the region as a veil adorns the face of a young woman. I gazed at the teeming waves and listened to their praise of God and meditated upon the eternal power hidden within them—that power which runs with the tempest and rises with the volcano and smiles through the lips of the roses and sings with the brooks.

Then I saw three phantoms sitting upon a rock. I stumbled toward them as if some power were pulling me against my will.

Within a few paces from the phantoms, I halted as though held still by a magic force. At that moment one of the phantoms stood up and in a voice that seemed to rise from the depth of the sea said:

"Life without Love is like a tree without blossom and fruit. And love without Beauty is like flowers without scent and fruits without seeds.... Life, Love, and Beauty are three persons in one, who cannot be separated or changed."

A second phantom spoke with a voice that roared like cascading water and said:

"Life without Rebellion is like seasons without Spring. And Rebellion without Right is like Spring in an arid desert.... Life, Rebellion, and Right are three-in-one who cannot be changed or separated."

Then the third phantom in a voice like a clap of thunder spoke:

"Life without Freedom is like a body without a soul, ant Freedom without Thought is like a confused spirit.... Life, Freedom, and Thought are three-in-one, and are everlasting and never pass away."

Then the three phantoms stood up together, and with one tremendous voice said:

"That which Love begets,
That which Rebellion creates,
That which Freedom rears,
Are three manifestations of God.
And God is the expression
Of the intelligent Universe."

At that moment Silence mingled with the rustling of invisible wings and trembling of ethereal bodies; and it prevailed.

I closed my eyes and listened to the echoes of the sayings which I had just heard, and when I opened them I saw nothing but the sea wreathed in mist. I walked toward the rock where the three phantoms were sitting, but I saw naught save a column of incense spiralling toward heaven.

21

EARTH

How beautiful you are, Earth, and how sublime!
How perfect is your obedience to the light, and
how noble is your submission to the sun!

How lovely you are, veiled in shadow, and how
charming your face, masked with obscurity!

How soothing is the song of your dawn, and how
harsh are the praises of your eventide!
How perfect you are, Earth, and how majestic!

I have walked over your plains, I have climbed your
stony mountains; I have descended into your valleys;
I have entered into your caves.
In the plains, I found your dream; upon the mountain
I found your pride; in the valley I witnessed your
tranquility; in the rocks your resolution; in the
cave your secrecy.

You are weak and powerful and humble and haughty.
You are pliant and rigid, and clear and secret.
I have ridden your seas and explored your rivers and

followed your brooks.
I heard Eternity speak through your ebb and flow, and the ages echoing your songs among your hills.
I listened to life calling to life in your mountain passes and along your slopes.
You are the mouth and lips of Eternity, the strings and fingers of Time, the mystery and solution of Life.
Your Spring has awakened me and led me to your fields where your aromatic breath ascends like incense.
I have seen the fruits of your Summer labor.
In Autumn, in your vineyards, I saw your blood flow as wine.
Your Winter carried me into your bed, where the snow attested your purity.
In your Spring you are an aromatic essence; in your Summer you are generous; in your Autumn you are a source of plenty.

One calm and clear night I opened the windows and doors of my soul and went out to see you, my heart tense with lust and greed.
And I saw you staring at the stars that smiled at you. So I cast away my fetters, for I found out that the dwelling place of the soul is in your space.
Its desires grow in your desires; its peace rests in your peace; and its happiness is in the golden dust which the stars sprinkle upon your body.

One night, as the skies turned gray, and my soul was wearied and anxious, I went out to you.
And you appeared to me like a giant, armed with

raging tempests, fighting the past with the present,
replacing the old with the new, and letting the
strong disperse the weak.

Whereupon I learned that the law of the people is
your law.
I learned that he who does not break his dry branches
with his tempest, will die wearily,
And he who does not use revolution, to strip
his dry leaves, will slowly perish.

How generous you are, Earth, and how strong is your
yearning for your children lost between that which
they have attained and that which they could not
obtain.
We clamor and you smile; we flit
but you stay!

We blaspheme and you consecrate.
We defile and you sanctify.
We sleep without dreams; but you
dream in your eternal wakefulness.

We pierce your bosom with swords and spears,
And you dress our wounds with oil and balsam.
We plant your fields with skulls and bones,
and from them you rear cypress
and willow trees.

We empty our wastes in your bosom, and you fill
our threshing-floors with wheat sheaves, and
our winepresses with grapes.

We extract your elements to make cannons and

bombs, but out of our elements you create
lilies and roses.

How patient you are, Earth, and how merciful!
Are you an atom of dust raised by
the feet of God when He journeyed from the east
to the west of the Universe?
Or a spark projected from the furnace
of Eternity?
Are you a seed dropped in the field of the
firmament to become God's tree reaching above
the heavens with its celestial branches?
Or are you a drop of blood in the veins of the
giant of giants, or a bead of sweat upon his
brow?

Are you a fruit ripened by the sun?
Do you grow from the tree of Absolute
Knowledge, whose roots extend through
Eternity, and whose branches soar through
the Infinite?

Are you a jewel placed by the God of Time in the
palm of the God of Space?

Who are you, Earth, and what are you?
You are "I," Earth!

You are my sight and my discernment.
You are my knowledge and my
dream
You are my hunger and my thirst.
You are my sorrow and my joy.
You are my inadvertence and my wakefulness.

EARTH

You are the beauty that lives in my eyes,
the longing in my heart, the everlasting life
in my soul.

You are "I," Earth.
Had it not been for my being,
You would not have been.

22

The Cry of the Graves

I

The Emir walked into the court room and took the central chair while at his right and left sat the wise men of the country. The guards, armed with swords and spears, stood in attention, and the people who came to witness the trial rose and bowed ceremoniously to the Emir whose eyes emanated a power that revealed horror to their spirits and fear to their hearts. As the court came to order and the hour of judgment approached, the Emir raised his hand and shouted saying, "Bring forth the criminals singly and tell me what crimes they have committed." The prison door opened like the mouth of a ferocious yawning beast. In the obscure corners of the dungeon one could hear the echo of shackles rattling in unison with the moaning and lamentations of the prisoners. The spectators were eager to see the prey of Death emerging from the depths of that inferno. A few moments later, two soldiers came out leading a young man with his arms pinioned behind his back. His stern face bespoke nobility of spirit and strength of the heart. He was halted in the middle of the court room and the soldiers marched a few steps to the rear. The Emir stared at him steadily and said, "What crime has this man, who is proudly and triumphantly standing before me, committed?" One of the courtmen responded, "He is a murderer; yesterday he slew one of the Emir's officers who was on an important mission in the surrounding villages; he was still grasping the bloody sword when he was arrested." The Emir retorted with anger, "Return the man to the dark prison and tie him with heavy chains, and at dawn cut off his head with his own sword and throw his body in the woods so that the beasts may eat the flesh, and the air may carry its remindful odor into the noses of his family and friends." The youth was returned to prison while the people looked upon him with sorrowful eyes, for he was a young man in the spring of life.

The soldiers returned back again from the prison leading a young woman of natural and frail beauty. She looked pale and upon her face appeared the signs of oppression and disappointment. Her eyes were soaked with tears and her head was bent under the burden of grief. After eyeing her thoroughly, the Emir exclaimed, "And this emaciated woman, who is standing before me like the shadow beside a corpse, what has she done?" One of the soldiers answered him, saying, "She is an adulteress; last night her husband discovered her in the arms of another. After her lover escaped, her husband turned her over to the law." The Emir looked at her while she raised her face without expression, and he ordered, "Take her back to the dark room and stretch her upon a bed of thorns so she may remember the resting place which she polluted with her fault; give her vinegar mixed with gall to drink so she may remember the taste of those sweet kisses. At dawn drag her naked body outside the city and stone her. Let the wolves enjoy the tender meat of her body and the worms pierce her bones." As she walked back to the dark cell, the people looked upon her with sympathy and surprise. They were astonished with the Emir's justice and grieved over her fate. The soldiers reappeared, bringing with them a sad man with shaking knees and trembling like a tender sapling before the north wind. He looked powerless, sickly and frightened, and he was miserable and poor. The Emir stared at him loathfully and inquired, "And this filthy man, who is like dead amongst the living; what has he done?" One of the guards returned, "He is a thief who broke into the monastery and stole the sacred vases which the priests found under his garment when they arrested him."

As a hungry eagle who looks at a bird with broken wings, the Emir looked at him and said, "Take him back to the jail and chain him, and at dawn drag him into a lofty tree and hang him between heaven and earth so his sinful hands may perish and the members of his body may be turned into particles and scattered by the wind." As the thief stumbled back into the depths of the prison, the people commenced whispering one to another saying, "How dare such a weak and heretic man steal the sacred vases of the monastery?"

At this time the court adjourned and the Emir walked out accompanied by all his wise men, guarded by the soldiers, while the audience scattered and the place became empty except of the moaning and wailing of the prisoners. All this happened while I was standing there like a mirror before passing ghosts. I was meditating the laws, made by man for man, contemplating what the people call "justice," and engrossing myself with deep thoughts of the secrets of life. I tried to understand the meaning of the universe. I was dumbfounded in finding myself lost like a horizon that disappears beyond the cloud. As I left the place I said to myself, "The vegetable feeds upon the elements of the earth, the sheep eats the vegetable, the wolf preys upon the sheep, and the bull kills the wolf while the lion devours the bull; yet Death claims the lion. Is there any power that will overcome. Death and make these brutalities an eternal justice? Is there a force that can convert all the ugly things into beautiful objects? Is there any might that can clutch with its hands all the elements of life and embrace them with joy as the sea joyfully engulfs all the brooks into its depths? Is there any power that can arrest the murdered and the murderer, the adulteress and the adulterer, the robber and the robbed, and bring them to a court loftier and more supreme than the court of the Emir?"

II

The next day I left the city for the fields where silence reveals to the soul that which the spirit desires, and where the pure sky kills the germs of despair, nursed in the city by the narrow streets and obscured places. When I reached the valley, I saw a flock of crows and vultures soaring and descending, filling the sky with cawing, whistling and rustling of the wings. As I proceeded I saw before me a corpse of a man hanged high in a tree, the body of a dead naked woman in the midst of a heap of stones, and a carcass of a youth with his head cut off and soaked with blood mixed with earth. It was a horrible sight that blinded my eyes with a thick, dark veil of sorrows. I looked in every direction and saw naught except the spectre of Death standing by those ghastly remains. Nothing could be heard except the wailing of nonexistence, mingled with the cawing of crows hovering about the victims of human laws. Three human beings, who yesterday were in the lap of Life, today fell as victims to Death because they broke the rules of human society. When a man kills another man, the people say he is a murderer, but when the Emir kills him, the Emir is just. When a man robs a monastery, they say he is a thief, but when the Emir robs him of his life, the Emir is honorable. When a woman betrays her husband, they say she is an adulteress, but when the Emir makes her walk naked in the streets and stones her later, the Emir is noble. Shedding of blood is forbidden, but who made it lawful for the Emir? Stealing one's money is a crime, but taking away one's life is a noble act. Betrayal of a husband may be an ugly deed, but stoning of living souls is a beautiful sight. Shall we meet evil with evil and say this the Law? Shall we fight corruption with greater corruption and say this is the Rule? Shall we conquer crimes with more crimes and say this is Justice? Had not the Emir killed an enemy in his past life? Had he not robbed his weak subjects of money and property? Had he not committed adultery? Was he infallible when he killed the murderer and hanged the thief and stoned the adulteress? Who are those who hanged the thief in the tree? Are they angels descended from heaven, or men looting and usurping? Who cut off the murderer's head? Are they divine prophets, or soldiers shedding blood wherever they go? Who stoned that adulteress? Were they virtuous hermits who came from their monasteries, or humans who loved to commit atrocities with glee, under the protection of ignorant Law? What is Law? Who saw it coming with the sun from the depths of heaven? What human saw the heart of God and found its will or purpose? In what century did the angels walk among the people and preach to them, saying, "Forbid the weak from enjoying life, and kill the outlaws with the sharp edge of the sword, and step upon the sinners with iron feet?"

As my mind suffered in this fashion, I heard a rustling

of feet in the grass close by. I took heed and saw a young woman coming from behind the trees; she looked carefully in every direction before she approached the three carcasses that were there. As she glanced, she saw the youth's head that was cut off. She cried fearfully, knelt, and embraced it with her trembling arms; then she commenced shedding tears and touching the blood-matted, curly hair with her soft fingers, crying in a voice that came from the remnants of a shattered heart. She could bear the sight no longer. She dragged the body to a ditch and placed the head gently between the shoulders, covered the entire body with earth, and upon the grave she planted the sword with which the head of the young man had been cut off.

As she started to leave, I walked toward her. She trembled when she saw me, and her eyes were heavy with tears. She sighed and said, "Turn me over to the Emir if you wish; It is better for me to die and follow the one who saved my life from the grip of disgrace than to leave his corpse as food for the ferocious beasts." Then I responded, "Fear me not, poor girl, I have lamented the young man before you did. But tell me, how did he save you from the grip of disgrace?" She replied with a choking and fainting voice, "One of the Emir's officers came to our farm to collect the tax; when he saw me, he looked upon me as a wolf looks upon a lamb. He imposed on my father a heavy tax that even a rich man could not pay. He arrested me as a token to take to the Emir in ransom for the gold which my father was unable to give. I begged him to spare me, but he took no heed, for he had no mercy. Then I cried for help, and this young man who is dead now, came to my help and saved me from a living death. The officer attempted to kill him, but this man took an old sword that was hanging on the wall of our home and stabbed him. He did not run away like a criminal, but stood by the dead officer until the law came and took him into custody." Having uttered these words which would make any human heart bleed with sorrow, she turned her face and walked away.

In a few moments I saw a youth coming and hiding his face with a cloak. As he approached the corpse of the adulteress, he took off the garment and placed it upon her naked body. Then he drew a dagger from under the cloak and dug a pit in which he placed the dead girl with tenderness and care, and covered her with earth upon which he poured his tears. When he finished his task, he plucked some flowers and placed them reverently upon the grave. As he started to leave, I halted him saying, "What kin are you to this adulteress? And what prompted you to endanger your life by coming here to protect her naked body from the ferocious beasts?" When he stared at me, his sorrowful eyes bespoke his misery, and he said, "I am the unfortunate man for whose love she was stoned; I loved her and she loved me since childhood; we grew together; Love, whom we served and revered, was the lord of our hearts. Love joined both of us and embraced our souls. One day I absented myself from the city, and upon my return I discovered that her father obliged her to marry a man she did not love. My life became a perpetual struggle, and all my days were converted into one long and dark night. I tried to be at peace with my heart, but my heart would not be still. Finally I went to see her secretly and my sole purpose was to have a glimpse of her beautiful eyes and hear the sound of her serene voice. When I reached her house I found her lonely, lamenting her unfortunate self. I sat by her; silence was our important conversation and virtue our companion. One hour of understanding quiet passed, when her husband entered. I cautioned him to contain himself but he dragged her with both hands into the street and cried out saying, "Come, come and see the adulteress and her lover!" All the neighbours rushed about and later the law came and took her to the Emir, but I was not touched by the soldiers. The ignorant Law and sodden customs punished the woman for her father's fault and pardoned the man."

Having thus spoken, the man turned toward the city while I remained pondering the corpse of the thief hanging in that lofty tree and moving slightly every time the wind shook the branches, waiting for some one to bring him down and stretch him upon the bosom of the earth beside the Defender of Honor and Martyr of Love. An hour later, a frail and wretched woman appeared, crying. She stood before the hanged man and prayed reverently. Then she struggled up into the tree and gnawed with her teeth on the linen rope until it broke and the dead fell on the ground like a huge wet cloth; whereupon she came down, dug a grave, and buried the thief by the side of the other two victims. After covering him with earth, she took two pieces of wood and fashioned a cross and placed it over the head. When she turned her face to the city and started to depart, I stopped her saying, "What incited you to come and bury this thief?" She looked at me miserably and said? "He is my faithful husband and merciful companion; he is the father of my children—five young ones starving to death; the oldest is eight years of age, and the youngest is still nursing. My husband was not a thief, but a farmer working in the monastery's land, making our living on what little food the priests and monks gave him when he returned home at eventide. He had been farming for them since he was young, and when he became weak, they dismissed him, advising him to go back home and send his children to take his place as soon as they grew older. He begged them in the name of Jesus and the angels of heaven to let him stay, but they took no heed to his plea. They had no mercy on him nor on his starving children who were helplessly crying for food. He went to the city seeking employment, but in vain, for the rich did not employ except the strong and the healthy. Then he sat on the dusty street stretching his hand toward all who passed, begging and repeating the sad song of his defeat in life, while suffering from hunger and humiliation, but the people refused to help him, saying that lazy people did not deserve alms. One night, hunger gnawed painfully at our children, especially the youngest, who tried hopelessly to nurse on my dry breast. My husband's expression changed and he left the house under the cover of night. He entered the monastery's bin and carried out a bushel of wheat. As he emerged, the monks woke up from their slumber and arrested him after beating him mercilessly. At dawn they brought him. to the Emir and complained that he came to the monastery to steal the golden vases of the altar. He was placed in prison and hanged the second day. He was trying to fill the stomachs of his little hungry ones with the wheat he had raised by his own labour, but the Emir killed him and used his flesh as food to fill the stomachs of the birds and the beasts." Having spoken in this manner, she left me alone in a sorrowful plight and departed.

I stood there before the graves like a speaker suffering wordlessness while trying to recite a eulogy. I was speechless, but my falling tears substituted for my words and spoke for my soul. My spirit rebelled when I attempted to meditate a while, because the soul is like a flower that folds its petals when dark comes, and breathes not its fragrance into the phantoms of the night. I felt as if the earth that enfolded the victims of oppression in that lonely place were filling my ears with sorrowful tunes of suffering souls, and inspiring me to talk. I resorted to silence, but if the people understood what silence reveals to them, they would have been as close to God as the flowers of the valleys. If the flames of my sighing soul had touched the trees, they would have moved from their places and marched like a strong army to fight the Emir with their branches and tear down the monastery upon the heads of those priests and monks. I stood there watching, and felt that the sweet feeling of mercy and the bitterness of sorrow were pouring from my heart upon the newly dug graves—a grave of a young man who sacrificed his life in defending a weak maiden, whose life and honor he had saved from between the paws and teeth of a savage human; a youth whose head was cut off in reward for his bravery; and his sword was planted upon his grave by the one he saved, as a symbol of heroism before the face of the sun that shines upon an empire laden with stupidity and corruption. A grave of a young woman whose heart was inflamed with love before her body was taken by greed, usurped by lust, and stoned by tyranny.... She kept her faith until death; her lover placed flowers upon her grave to speak through their withering hours of those souls whom Love had selected and blessed among a people blinded by earthly substance and muted by ignorance. A grave of a miserable man, weakened by hard labour in the monastery's land, who asked for bread to feed his hungry little ones, and was refused. He resorted to begging, but the people took no heed. When his soul led him to restore a small part of the crop which he had raised and gathered, he was arrested and beaten to death. His poor widow erected a cross upon his head as a witness in the silence of the night before the stars of heaven to testify against those priests who converted the kind teaching of Christ into sharp swords by which they cut the people's necks and tore the bodies of the weak.

The sun disappeared behind the horizon as if tiring of the world's troubles and loathing the people's submission. At that moment the evening began to weave a delicate veil from the sinews of silence and spread it upon Nature's body. I stretched my hand toward the graves, pointing at their symbols, lifted my eyes toward heaven and cried out, "Oh, Bravery, this is your sword, buried now in the earth! Oh, Love, these are your flowers, scorched by fire! Oh, Lord Jesus, this is Thy Cross, submerged in the obscurity of the night!"

23

KHALIL THE HERETIC

I

Sheik Abbas was looked upon as a prince by the people of a solitary village in North Lebanon. His mansion stood in the midst of those poor villagers' huts like a healthy giant amidst sickly dwarfs. He lived amid luxury while they pursued an existence of penury. They obeyed him and bowed reverently before him as he spoke to them. It seemed as though the power of mind had appointed him its official interpreter and spokesman. His anger would make them tremble and scatter like autumn leaves before a strong wind. If he were to slap one's face, it would be heresy on the individual's part to move or lift his head or make any attempt to discover why the blow had come. If he smiled at a man, the villagers would consider the person thus honoured as the most fortunate. The people's fear and surrender to Sheik Abbas were not due to weakness; however, their poverty and need of him had brought about this state of continual humiliation. Even the huts they lived in and the fields they cultivated were owned by Sheik Abbas who had inherited them from his ancestors.

The farming of the land and the sowing of the seeds and the gathering of wheat were all done under the supervision of the Sheik who, in reward for their toil, compensated them with a small portion of the crop which barely kept them from falling as victims of gnawing starvation.

Often many of them were in need of bread before the crop was reaped, and they came to Sheik Abbas and asked him with pouring tears to advance them a few piastres or a bushel of wheat, and the Sheik gladly granted their request for he knew that they would pay their debts doubly when harvest time came. Thus those people remained obligated all their lives, left a legacy of debts to their children and were submissive to their master whose anger they had always feared and whose friendship and good will they had constancy but unsuccessfully endeavoured to win.

II

Winter came and brought heavy snow and strong winds; the valleys and the fields became empty of all things except leafless trees which stood as spectres of death above the lifeless plains.

Having stored the products of the land in the Sheik's bins and filled his vases with the wine of the vineyards, the villagers retreated to their huts to spend a portion of their lives idling by the fireside and commemorating the glory of the past ages and relating to one another the tales of weary days and long nights.

The old year had just breathed its last into the grey sky. The night had arrived during which the New Year would be crowned and placed upon the Throne of the Universe. The snow began to fall heavily and the whistling winds were racing from the lofty mountains down to the abyss and blowing the snow into heaps to be stored away in the valleys.

The trees were shaking under the heavy storms and the fields and knolls were covered with a white floor upon which Death was writing vague lines and effacing them. The mists stood as partitions between the scattered villages by the sides of the valleys. The lights that flickered through the windows of those wretched huts disappeared behind the thick veil of Nature's wrath.

Fear penetrated the fellahin's hearts and the animals stood by their mangers in the sheds, while the dogs were hiding in the corners. One could hear the voices of the screaming winds and thundering of the storms resounding from the depths of the valleys. It seemed as if Nature were enraged by the passing of the old year and trying to wrest revenge from those peaceful souls by fighting with weapons of cold and frost.

That night under the raging sky, a young man was attempting to walk the winding trail that connected Deir Kizhaya* with Sheik Abbas's village. The youth's limbs were numbed with cold, while pain and hunger usurped him of his strength. The black raiment he wore was bleached with the falling snow, as if he were shrouded in death before the hour of his death had come. He was struggling against the wind. His progress was difficult, and he took but a few steps forward with each effort. He called for help and then stood silent, shivering in the cold night. He had slim hope, withering between great despair and deep sorrow. He was

---

*One of the richest and most famous convents in Lebanon. Kizhaya is a Syrian word meaning "Paradise of Life." [Editor's note.]

like a bird with a broken wing, who fell in a stream whose whirlpools carried him down to the depths.

The young man continued walking and falling until his blood stopped circulating and he collapsed. He uttered a terrible sound...the voice of a soul who encountered the hollow face of Death...a voice of dying youth, weakened by man and trapped by nature...a voice of the love of existence in the space of nothingness.

III

On the north side of that village, in the midst of the wind-torn fields, stood the solitary home of a woman named Rachel, and her daughter Miriam who had not then attained the age of eighteen. Rachel was the widow of Samaan Ramy, who was found slain six years earlier, but the law of man did not find the murderer.

Like the rest of the Lebanese widows, Rachel sustained life through long, hard work. During the harvest season, she would look for ears of corn left behind by others in the fields, and in Autumn she gathered the remnants of some forgotten fruits in the gardens. In Winter she spun wool and made raiment for which she received a few piastres or a bushel of grain. Miriam, her daughter, was a beautiful girl who shared with her mother the burden of toil.

That bitter night the two women were sitting by the fireplace whose warmth was weakened by the frost and whose firebrands were buried beneath the ashes. By their side was a flickering lamp that sent its yellow, dimmed rays into the heart of darkness like prayer that sends phantoms of hope into the hearts of the sorrowful.

Midnight had come and they were listening to the wailing winds outside. Every now and then Miriam would get up, open the small transom and look toward the obscured sky, and then she would return to her chair worried and frightened by the raging elements. Suddenly Miriam started, as if she had awakened from a swoon of deep slumber. She looked anxiously toward her mother and said, "Did you hear that, Mother? Did you hear a voice calling for help?" The mother listened a moment and said, "I hear nothing except the crying wind, my daughter." Then Miriam exclaimed, "I heard a voice deeper than the thundering heaven and more sorrowful than the wailing of the tempest."

Having uttered these words, she stood up and opened the door and listened for a moment. Then she said, "I hear it again, Mother!" Rachel hurried toward the frail door and after a moment's hesitation she said, "And I hear it, too. Let us go and see."

She wrapped herself with a long robe, opened the door and walked out cautiously, while Miriam stood at the door, the wind blowing her long hair.

Having forced her way a short distance through the snow, Rachel stopped and shouted out, "Who is calling...where are you?" There was no answer; then she repeated the same words again and again, but she heard naught except thunder. Then she courageously advanced forward, looking in every direction. She had walked for some time, when she found some deep footprints upon the snow; she followed them fearfully and in a few moments found a human body lying before her on the snow, like a patch on a white dress. As she approached him and leaned his head over her knees, she felt his pulse that bespoke his slowing heart beats and his slim chance in life. She turned her face toward the hut and called, "Come, Miriam, come and help me, I have found him!" Miriam rushed out and followed her mother's footprints, while shivering with cold and trembling with fear. As she reached the place and saw the youth lying motionless, she cried with an aching voice. The mother put her hands under his armpits, calmed Miriam and said, "Fear not, for he is still living; hold the lower edge of his cloak and let us carry him home."

Confronted with the strong wind and heavy snow, the two women carried the youth and started toward the hut. As they reached the little haven, they laid him down by the fireplace. Rachel commenced rubbing his numbed hands and Miriam drying his hair with the end of her dress. The youth began to move after a few minutes. His eyelids quivered and he took a deep sigh—a sigh that brought the hope of his safety into the hearts of the merciful women. They removed his shoes and took off his black robe. Miriam looked at her mother and said, "Observe his raiment, Mother; these clothes are worn by the monks." After feeding the fire with a bundle of dry sticks, Rachel looked at her daughter with perplexity and said, "The monks do not leave their convent on such a terrible night." And Miriam inquired, "But he has no hair on his face; the monks wear beards." The mother gazed at him with eyes full of mercy and maternal love; then she turned to her daughter and said, "It makes no difference whether he is a monk or criminal; dry his feet well, my daughter." Rachel opened a closet, took from it a jar of wine and poured some in an earthenware bowl. Miriam held his head while the mother gave him some of it to stimulate his heart. As he sipped the wine he opened his eyes for the first time and gave his rescuers a sorrowful look mingled with tears of gratitude—the look of a human who felt the smooth touch of life after having been gripped in the sharp claws of death—a look of great hope after hope had died. Then he bent his head, and his lips trembled when he uttered the words, "May God bless both of you." Rachel placed her hand upon his shoulder and said, "Be calm, brother. Do not tire yourself with talking until you gain strength." And Miriam added, "Rest four head on this pillow, brother, and we will place you closer to the fire." Rachel refilled the bowl with wine and gave it to him. She looked at her daughter and said, "Hang his robe by the fire so it will dry." Having executed her mother's command, she returned and commenced looking at him mercifully, as if she wanted to help him by pouring into his heart all the warmth of her soul. Rachel brought two loaves of bread with some preserves and dry fruits; she sat by him and began to feed him small morsels, as a mother feeds her little child. At this time he felt stronger and sat up on the hearth mat while the red flames of fire reflected upon his sad face. His eyes brightened and he shook his head slowly, saying, "Mercy and cruelty are both wrestling in the human heart like the mad elements in the sky of this terrible night, but mercy shall overcome cruelty because it is divine, and the terror alone, of this night, shall pass away when daylight comes." Silence prevailed for a minute and then he added with a whispering voice, "A human hand drove me into desperation and a human hand rescued me; how severe man is, and how merciful man is! And Rachel inquired, "How ventured you, brother, to leave the convent on such a terrible night, when even the beasts do not venture forth?"

The youth shut his eyes as if he wanted to restore his tears back into the depths of his heart, whence they came, and he said, "The animals have their caves, and the birds of the sky their nests, but the son of man has no place to rest his head." Rachel retorted, "That is what Jesus said about himself" And the young man resumed, "This is the answer for every man who wants to follow the Spirit and the Truth in this age of falsehood, hypocrisy and corruption."

After a few moments of contemplation, Rachel said, "But there are many comfortable rooms in the convent, and the coffers are full of gold, and all kinds of provisions. The sheds of the convent are stocked with fat calves and sheep; what made you leave such haven in this deathly night?" The youth sighed deeply and said, "I left that place because I hated it." And Rachel rejoined, "A monk in a convent is like a soldier in the battlefield who is required to obey the orders of his leader regardless of their nature. I heard that a man could not become a monk unless he did away with his will, his thought, his desires, and all that pertains to the mind. But a good head priest does not ask his monks to do unreasonable things. How could the head priest of Deir Kizhaya ask you to give up your life to the storms and snow?" And he remarked, "In the opinion of the head priest, a man cannot become a monk unless he is blind and ignorant, senseless and dumb. I left the convent because I am a sensible man who can see, feel, and hear."

Miriam and Rachel stared at him as if they had found in his face a hidden secret; after a moment of meditation the mother said, "Will a man who sees and hears go out on a night that blinds the eyes and deafens the ears?" And the youth stated quietly, "I was expelled from the convent." "Expelled !" exclaimed Rachel; and Miriam repeated the same word in unison with her mother.

He lifted his head, regretting his words, for he was afraid lest their love and sympathy be converted into hatred and disrespect; but when he looked at them and found the rays of mercy still emanating from their eyes, and their bodies vibrating with anxiety to learn further, his voice choked and he continued, "Yes, I was expelled from the convent because I could not dig my grave with my own hands, and my heart grew weary of lying and pilfering. I was expelled from the convent because my soul refused to enjoy the bounty of a people who surrendered themselves to ignorance. I was driven away because I could not find rest in the comfortable rooms, built with the money of the poor fellahin. My stomach could not hold bread baked with the tears of orphans. My lips could not utter prayers sold for gold and food by the heads to the simple and faithful people. I was expelled from the convent like a filthy leper because I was repeating to the monks the rules that qualified them to their present position."

Silence prevailed while Rachel and Miriam were contemplating his words and gazing at him, when they asked, "Are your father and mother living?" And he responded, "I have no father or mother nor a place that is my home." Rachel drew a deep sigh and Miriam turned her face toward the wall to hide her merciful and loving tears.

As a withering flower is brought back to life by dew drops that dawn pours into its begging petals, so the youth's anxious heart was enlivened by his benefactors' affection and kindness. He looked at them as a soldier looks upon his liberators who rescue him from the grip of the enemy, and he resumed, "I lost my parents before I reached the age of seven. The village priest took me to Deir Kizhaya and left me at the disposal of the monks who were happy to take me in and put me in charge of the cows and sheep, which I led each day to the pasture. When I attained the age of fifteen, they put on me this black robe and led me into the altar whereupon the head priest addressed me saying, "Swear by the name of God and all saints, and make a vow to live a virtuous life of poverty and obedience." I repeated the words before I realized their significance or comprehended his own interpretation of poverty, virtue and obedience.

My name was Khalil, and since that time the monks addressed me as Brother Mobaarak,* but they never did treat me as a brother. They ate the most palatable foods and drank the finest wine, while I lived on dry vegetables and water, mixed with tears. They slumbered in soft beds while I slept on a stone slab in a dark and cold room by the shed. Oftentimes I asked myself, "When will I become a monk and share with those fortunate priests their bounty? When will my heart stop craving for the food they eat and the wine they drink? When will I cease to tremble with fear before my superior?" But all my hopes were in vain, for I was kept in the same state; and in addition to caring for the cattle, I was obliged to move heavy stones on my shoulders and to dig pits and ditches. I sustained life on a few morsels of bread given to me in reward for my toil. I knew of no other place to which I might go, and the clergymen at the convent had caused me to abhor everything they were doing. They had poisoned my mind until I commenced to think that the whole world was an ocean of sorrows and miseries and that the convent was the only port of salvation. But when I discovered the source of their food and gold, I was happy that I did not share it."

Khalil straightened himself and looked about with wonder, as if he had found something beautiful standing before him in that wretched hut. Rachel and Miriam remained silent and he proceeded, "God, who took my father and exiled me as an orphan to the convent, did not

---

*Coincidentally, Mobaarak was the name of the Right Reverend Maronite Archbishop who officiated at Kahlil Gibran's last rites. (Editor's Note.)

want me to spend all my life walking blindly toward a dangerous jungle; nor did He wish me to be a miserable slave for the rest of my life. God opened my eyes and ears and showed me the bright light and made me hear Truth when Truth was talking."

Rachel thought aloud, "Is there any light, other than the sun, that shines over all the people? Are human beings capable of understanding the Truth?" Khalil returned, "The true light is that which emanates from within man, and reveals the secrets of the heart to the soul, making it happy and contented with life. Truth is like the stars; it does not appear except from behind obscurity of the night. Truth is like all beautiful things in the world; it does not disclose its desirability except to those who first feel the influence of falsehood. Truth is a deep kindness that teaches us to be content in our everyday life and share with the people the same happiness."

Rachel rejoined, "Many are those who live according to their goodness, and many are those who believe that compassion to others is the shadow of the law of God to man; but still, they do not rejoice in life, for they remain miserable until death." Khalil replied, "Vain are the beliefs and teachings that make man miserable, and false is the goodness that leads him into sorrow and despair, for it is man's purpose to be happy on this earth and lead the way to felicity and preach its gospel wherever he goes. He who does not see the kingdom of heaven in this life will never see it in the coming life. We came not into this life by exile, but we came as innocent creatures of God, to learn how to worship the holy and eternal spirit and seek the hidden secrets within ourselves from the beauty of life. This is the truth which I have learned from the teachings of the Nazarene. This is the light that came from within me and showed me the dark corners of the convent that threatened my life. This is the deep secret which the beautiful valleys and fields revealed to me when I was hungry, sitting lonely and weeping under the shadow of the trees.

This is the religion as the convent should impart it; as God wished it; as Jesus taught it. One day, as my soul became intoxicated with the heavenly intoxication of Truth's beauty, I stood bravely before the monks who were gathering in the garden, and criticized their wrong deeds saying, 'Why do you spend your days here and enjoy the bounty of the poor, whose bread you eat was made with the sweat of their bodies and the tears of their hearts? Why are you living in the shadow of parasitism, segregating yourselves from the people who are in need of knowledge? Why are you depriving the country of your help? Jesus has sent you as lambs amongst the wolves; what has made you as wolves amongst the lambs? Why are you fleeing from mankind and from God who created you? If you are better than the people who walk in the procession of life, you should go to them and better their lives; but if you think they arc better than you, you should desire to learn from them. How do you take an oath and vow to live in poverty, then forget what you have said and live in luxury? How do you swear an obedience to God and then revolt against all that religion means? How do you adopt virtue as your rule when your heart is full of lusts? You pretend that you are killing your bodies, but in fact you are killing your souls. You feign to abhor the earthly things, but your heart is swollen with greed. You have the people believe in you as a religious teacher; truly speaking you are like busy cattle who divert themselves from knowledge by grazing in a green and beautiful pasture. Let us restore to the needy the vast land of the convent and give back to them the silver and gold we took from them. Let us disperse from our aloofness and serve the weak who made us strong, and cleanse the country in which we live. Let us teach this miserable nation to smile and rejoice with heaven's bounty and glory of life and freedom.

"The people's tears are more beautiful and God-joined than the ease and tranquility to which you have accustomed yourselves in this place. The sympathy that touches the neighbour's heart is more supreme than the hidden virtue in the unseen corners of the convent. A word of compassion to the weak criminal or prostitute is nobler than the long prayer which we repeat emptily every day in the temple."

At this time Khalil took a deep breath. Then he lifted his eyes toward Rachel and Miriam saying, "I was saying all of these things to the monks and they were listening with an air of perplexity, as if they could not believe that a young man would dare stand before them and utter such bold words. When I finished, one of the monks approached and angrily said to me, 'How dare you talk in such fashion in our presence?' And another one came laughing and added, 'Did you learn all this from the cows and pigs you tended in the fields?' And a third one stood up and threatened me saying, 'You shall be punished, heretic!' Then they dispersed as though running away from a leper. Some of them complained to the head priest who summoned me before him at eventide. The monks took delight in anticipation of my suffering, and there was glee on their faces when I was ordered to be scourged and put into prison for forty days and nights. They led me into the dark cell where I spent the time lying in that grave without seeing the light. I could not tell the end of the night from the beginning of the day, and could feel nothing but crawling insects and the earth under me. I could hear naught save the tramping of the feet when my morsel of bread and dish of water mixed with vinegar were brought to me at great intervals.

When I came out of the prison I was weak and frail, and the monks believed that they had cured me of thinking, and that they had killed my soul's desire. They thought that hunger and thirst had choked the kindness which God placed in my heart. In my forty days of solitude I endeavoured to find a method by which I could help these monks to see the light and hear the true song of life, but all of my ponderings were in vain, for the thick veil which the long ages had woven around their eyes could not be torn away in a short time; and the mortar with which ignorance had cemented their ears was hardened and could not be removed by the touch of soft fingers."

Silence prevailed for a moment, and then Miriam looked at her mother as if asking her permission to let her talk. She said, "You must have talked to the monks again, if they selected this terrible night in which to banish you from the convent. They should learn to be kind even to their enemies."

Khalil returned, "This evening, as the thunder storms and warring elements raged in the sky, I withdrew myself from the monks who were crouching about the fire, telling tales and humorous stories. When they saw me alone they commenced to place their wit at my expense. I was reading my Gospel and contemplating the beautiful sayings of Jesus that made me forget for the time the enraged nature and belligerent elements of the sky, when they approached me with a new spirit of ridicule. I ignored them by occupying myself and looking through the window, but they became furious because my silence dried the laughter of their hearts and the taunting of their lips. One of them said, 'What are you reading, Great Reformer?' In response to his inquiry, I opened my book and read aloud the following passage, 'But when he saw many of the Pharisees and Saducees come to his baptism, he said unto them, "O generation of vipers, who hath warned you to flee from the wrath to come? Bring forth therefore fruits for repentance; And think not to say within yourselves, 'We have Abraham to our father;' for I say unto you, that God is able of these stones to raise children unto Abraham. And now also the axe is laid unto the root of the trees; therefore every tree which bringeth not forth good fruit is hewn down, and cast into the fire.'

"As I read to them these words of John the Baptist, the monies became silent as if an invisible hand strangled their spirits, but they took false courage and commenced laughing. One of them said, 'We have read these words many times, and we are not in need of a cow grazier to repeat them to us.'

"I protested, 'If you had read these words and comprehended their meaning, these poor villagers would not have frozen or starved to death.' When I said this, one of the monks slapped my face as if I had spoken evil of the priests; another kicked me and a third took the book from me and a fourth one called the head priest who hurried to the scene shaking with anger. He cried out, 'Arrest this rebel and drag him from this sacred place, and let the storm's fury teach him obedience. Take him away and let nature do unto him the will of God, and then wash your hands of the poisonous germs of heresy infesting his raiment. If he should return pleading for forgiveness, do not open the door for him, for the viper will not become a dove if placed in a cage, nor will the briar bear figs if planted in the vineyards.'

"In accordance with the command, I was dragged out by the laughing monks. Before they locked the door behind me, I heard one saying, 'Yesterday you were king of cows and pigs, and today you are dethroned, Oh Great Reformer; go now and be the king of wolves and teach them how to live in their lairs.'"

Khalil sighed deeply, then turned his face and looked toward the flaming fire. With a sweet and loving voice, and with a pained countenance he said, "Thus was I expelled from the convent, and thus did the monks deliver me over to the hands of Death. I fought through the night blindly; the heavy wind was tearing my robe and the piling snow was trapping my feet and pulling me down until I fell, crying desperately for help. I felt that no one heard me except Death, but a power which is all knowledge and mercy had heard my cry. That power did not want me to die before I had learned what is left of life's secrets. That power sent you both to me to save my life from the depth of the abyss and non-existence."

Rachel and Miriam felt as if their spirits understood the mystery of his soul, and they became his partners in feeling and understanding. Notwithstanding her will, Rachel stretched forth and gently touched his hand while tears coursed down from her eyes, and she said, "He who has been chosen by heaven as a defender of Truth will not perish by heaven's own storms and snow." And Miriam added, "The storms and snow may kill the flowers, but cannot deaden the seeds, for the snow keeps them warm from the killing frost."

Khalil's face brightened upon hearing those words of encouragement, and he said, "If you do not look upon me as a rebel and an heretic as the monks did, the persecution which I have sustained in the convent is the symbol of an oppressed nation that has not yet attained knowledge; and this night in which I was on the verge of death is like a revolution that precedes full justice. And from a sensitive woman's heart springs the happiness of mankind, and from the kindness of her noble spirit comes mankind's affection."

He closed his eyes and leaned down on the pillow; the two women did not bother him with further conversation for they knew that the weariness caused by long exposure had allured and captured his eyes. Khalil slept like a lost child who had finally found safety in his mother's arms.

Rachel and her daughter slowly walked to their bed and sat there watching him as if they had found in his trouble-torn face an attraction bringing their souls and hearts closer to him. And the mother whispered, saying, "There is a strange power in his closed eyes that speaks in silence and stimulates the soul's desires."

And Miriam rejoined, "His hands, Mother, are like those of Christ in the Church." The mother replied, "His face possesses at the same time a woman's tenderness and a man's boldness."

And the wings of slumber carried the women's spirits into the world of dream, and the fire went down and turned into ashes, while the light of the oil lamp dimmed gradually and disappeared. The fierce tempest continued its roar, and the obscured sky spread layers of snow, and the strong wind scattered them to the right and left.

IV

Five days passed, and the sky was still heavy with snow, burying the mountains and prairies relentlessly. Khalil made three attempts to resume his journey toward the plains, but Rachel restrained him each time, saying, "Do not give up your life to the blind elements, brother; remain here, for the bread that suffices two will also feed three, and the fire will still be burning after your departure as it was before your arrival. We are poor, brother, but like the rest of the people, we live our lives before the face of the sun and mankind, and God gives us our daily bread."

And Miriam was begging him with her kind glances, and pleading with her deep sighs, for since he entered the hut she felt the presence of a divine power in her soul sending forth life and light into her heart and awakening new affection in the Holy of Holies of her spirit. For the first time she experienced the feeling which made her heart like a white rose that sips the dew drops from the dawn and breathes its fragrance into the endless firmament.

There is no affection purer and more soothing to the spirit than the one hidden in the heart of a maiden who awakens suddenly and fills her own spirit with heavenly music that makes her days like poet's dreams and her nights prophetic. There is no secret in the mystery of life stronger and more beautiful than that attachment which converts the silence of a virgin's spirit into a perpetual awareness that makes a person forget the past, for it kindles fiercely in his heart the sweet and overwhelming hope of the coming future.

The Lebanese woman distinguishes herself from the woman of other nations by her simplicity. The manner in which she is trained restricts her progress educationally, and stands as a hindrance to her future. Yet for this reason, she finds herself inquiring of herself as to the inclination and mystery of her heart. The Lebanese young woman is like a spring that comes out from the heart of the earth and follows its course through winding depressions, but since it cannot find an outlet to the sea, it turns into a calm lake that reflects upon its growing surface the glittering stars and the shining moon. Khalil felt the vibration of Miriam's heart twining steadily about his soul, and he knew that the divine torch that illuminated his heart had also touched her heart. He rejoiced for the first time, like a parched brook greeting the rain, but he blamed himself for his haste, believing that this spiritual understanding would pass like a cloud when he departed from that village. He often spoke to himself saying, "What is this mystery that plays so great a part in our lives? What is this Law that drives us into a rough road and stops us just before we reach the face of the sun where we might rejoice? What is this power that elevates our spirits until we reach the mountain top, smiling and glorying, then suddenly we are cast to the depths of the valley, weeping and suffering? What is this life that embraces us like a lover one day, and fights us like an enemy the second day ? Was I not persecuted yesterday? Did I not survive hunger and thirst and suffering and mockery for the sake of the Truth which heaven had awakened in my heart? Did I not tell the monks that happiness through Truth is the will and the purpose of God in man? Then what is this fear? And why do I close my eyes to the light that emanates from that young woman's eyes? I am expelled and she is poor, but is it on bread only that man can live? Are we not, between famine and plenty, like trees between winter and summer? But what would Rachel say if she knew that my heart and her daughter's heart came to an understanding in silence, and approached close to each other and neared the circle of the Supreme Light? What would she say if she discovered that the young man whose life she saved longed to gaze upon her daughter? What would the simple villagers say if they knew that a young man, reared in the convent, came to their village by necessity and expulsion, and desired to live near a beautiful maiden? Will they listen to me if I tell them that he who leaves the convent to live amongst them is like a bird that flies from the bruising walls of the cage to the light of freedom? What will Sheik Abbas say if he hears my story? What will the priest of the village do if he learns of the cause for my expulsion?"

Khalil was talking to himself in this fashion while sitting by the fireplace, meditating the flames, symbol of his love; and Miriam was stealing a glance now and then at his face and reading his dreams through his eyes, and hearing the echo of his thoughts, and feeling the touch of his love, even though no word was uttered.

One night, as he stood by the small transom that faced the valleys where the trees and rocks were shrouded with white coverings, Miriam came and stood by him, looking at the sky. As their eyes turned and met, he drew a deep sigh and shut his eyes as if his soul were sailing in the spacious sky looking for a word. He found no word necessary, for the silence spoke for them. Miriam ventured, "Where will you go when the snow meets the stream and the paths are dry?" His eyes opened, looking beyond the horizon, and he explained, "I shall follow the path to wherever my destiny and my mission for Truth shall take me." Miriam sighed sadly and offered, "Why will you not remain here and live close to us? Is it that you are obliged to go elsewhere?" He was moved by her kindness and sweet words, but protested, "The villagers here will not accept an expelled monk as their neighbour, and will not permit him to breathe the air they breathe because they believe that the enemy of the convent is an infidel, cursed by God and his saints." Miriam resorted to silence, for the Truth that pained her prevented further talk. Then Khalil turned aside and explained "Miriam, these villagers are taught by those in authority to hate everyone who thinks freely; they are trained to remain afar from those whose minds soar aloft; God does not like to be worshipped by an ignorant man who imitates someone else; if I remained in this village and asked the people to worship as they please, they would say that I am an infidel disobeying the authority that was given to the priest by God. If I asked them to listen and hear the voices of their hearts and do according to the will of the spirit within, they would say that I am an evil man who wants them to do away with the clergy that Clod placed between heaven and earth." Khalil looked straight into Miriam's eyes, and with a voice that bespoke the sound of silver strings said, "But, Miriam, there is a magic power in this village that possesses me and engulfs my soul; a power so diving that it causes me to forget my pain. In this village I met Death to his very face, and in this place my soul embraced God's spirit. In this village there is a beautiful flower grown over the lifeless grass; its beauty attracts my heart and its fragrance fills its domain. Shall I leave this important flower and go out preaching the ideas that caused my expulsion from the convent, or shall I remain by the side of that flower and dig a grave and bury my thoughts and truths among its neighboring thorns? What shall I do, Miriam?" Upon hearing these words, she shivered like a lily before the frolicsome breeze of the dawn. Her heart glowed through her eyes when she faltered, "We are both in the hands of a mysterious and merciful power. Let it do its will."

At that moment the two hearts joined and there after both spirits were one burning torch illuminating their lives.

V

Since the beginning of the creation and up to our present

time, certain clans, rich by inheritance, in co-operation with the clergy, had appointed themselves the administrators of the people. It is an old, gaping wound in the heart of society that cannot be removed except by intense removal of ignorance.

The man who acquires his wealth by inheritance builds his mansion with the weak poor's money. The clergyman erects his temple upon the graves and bones of the devoted worshipers. The prince grasps the fellah's arms while the priest empties his pocket; the ruler looks upon the sons of the fields with frowning face, and the bishop consoles them with his smile, and between the frown of the tiger and the smile of the wolf the flock is perished; the ruler claims himself as king of the law, and the priest as the representative of God, and between these two, the bodies are destroyed and the souls wither into nothing.

In Lebanon, that mountain rich in sunlight and poor in knowledge, the noble and the priest joined hands to exploit the fanner who ploughed the land and reaped the crop in order to protect himself from the sword of the ruler and the curse of the priest. The rich man in Lebanon stood proudly by his palace and shouted at the multitudes saying, "The Sultan has appointed me as your lord." And the priest stands before the altar saying, "God has delegated me as an executive of your souls." But the Lebanese resorted to silence, for the dead could not talk.

Sheik Abbas had friendship in his heart for the clergymen, because they were his allies in choking the people's knowledge and reviving the spirit of stern obedience among his workers.

That evening, when Khalil and Miriam were approaching the throne of Love, and Rachel was looking upon them with the eyes of affection, Father Elias informed Sheik

Abbas that the head priest had expelled a rebellious young man from the convent and that he had taken refuge at the house of Rachel, the widow of Samaan Ramy. And the priest was not satisfied with the little information he gave the Sheik, but commented, "The demon they chased out of the convent cannot become an angel in this village, and the fig tree which is hewn and cast into the fire, does not bear fruit while burning. If we wish to clean this village of the filth of this beast, we must drive him away as the monks did." And the Sheik inquired, "Are you certain that the young man will be a bad influence upon our people? Is it not better for us to keep him and make him a worker in our vineyards? We are in need of strong men."

The priest's face showed his disagreement. Combing his beard with his fingers, he said shrewdly, "If he were fit to work, he would not have been expelled from the convent. A student who works in the convent, and who happened to spend last night at my house, informed me that this young man had violated the rules of the head priest by preaching danger-ridden ideas among the monks, and he quoted him as saying, 'Restore the fields and the vineyards and the silver of the convent to the poor and scatter it in all directions; and help the people who arc in need of knowledge; by thus doing, you will please your Father in Heaven.'"

On hearing these words, Sheik Abbas leaped to his feet, and like a tiger making ready to strike the victim, he walked to the door and called to the servants, ordering them to report immediately. Three men entered, and the Sheik commanded, "In the house of Rachel, the widow of Samaan Ramy, there is a young man wearing a monk's raiment. Tie him and bring him here. If that woman objects to his arrest, drag her out by her braided hair over the snow and bring her with him, for he who helps evil is evil himself." The men bowed obediently and hurried to Rachel's home while the priest and the Sheik discussed the type of punishment to be awarded to Khalil and Rachel.

VI

The day was over and the night had come spreading its shadow over those wretched huts, heavily laden with snow. The stars finally appeared in the sky, like hopes in the coming eternity after the suffering of death's agony. The doors and windows were closed and the lamps were lighted. The fellahin sat by the fireside warming their bodies. Rachel, Miriam and Khalil were seated at a rough wooden table eating their evening meal when there was a knock at the door and three men entered. Rachel and Miriam were frightened, but Khalil remained calm, as if he awaited the coming of those men. One of the Sheik's servants walked toward Khalil, laid his hand upon his shoulder and asked, "Are you the one who was expelled from the convent?" And Khalil responded, "Yes, I am the one, what do you want?" The man replied, "We are ordered to arrest you and take you with us to Sheik Abbas's home, and if you object we shall drag you out like a butchered sheep over the snow."

Rachel turned pale as she exclaimed, "What crime has he committed, and why do you want to tie him and drag him out?" The two women pleaded with tearful voices, saying, "He is one individual in the hands of three and it is cowardly of you to make him suffer." The men became enraged and shouted, "Is there any woman in this village who opposes the Sheik's order?" And he drew forth a rope and started to tie Khalil's hands. Khalil lifted his head proudly, and a sorrowful smile appeared on his lips when he said, "I feel sorry for you men, because you are a strong and blind instrument in the hands of a man who oppresses the weak with the strength of your arms. You are slaves of ignorance. Yesterday I was a man like you, but tomorrow you shall be free in mind as I am now. Between us there is a deep precipice that chokes my calling voice and hides my reality from you, and you cannot hear or see. Here I am, tie my hands and do as you please." The three men were moved by his talk and it seemed that his voice had awakened in them a new spirit, but the voice of Sheik Abbas still rang in their minds, warning them to complete the mission. They bound his hands and led him out silently with a heavy conscience. Rachel and Miriam followed them to the Sheik's home, like the daughters of Jerusalem who followed Christ to Mount Calvary.

VII

Regardless of its import, news travels swiftly among the fellahin in the small villages, because their absence from the realm of society makes them anxious and busy in discussing the happenings of their limited environs. In winter, when the fields are slumbering under the quilts of snow, and when human life is taking refuge and warming itself by the fireside, the villagers become most inclined to learn of current news in order to occupy themselves.

It was not long after Khalil was arrested, when the story spread like a contagious disease amongst the villagers. They left their huts and hurried like an army from every direction into the home of Sheik Abbas. When Khalil's feet stepped in the Sheik's home, the residence was crowded with men, women and children who were endeavouring for a glance at the infidel who was expelled from the convent. They were also anxious to see Rachel and her daughter, who had helped Khalil in spreading the hellish disease of heresy in the pure sky of their village.

The Sheik took the seat of judgment and beside him sat Father Elias, while the throng was gazing at the pinioned youth who stood bravely before them. Rachel and Miriam were standing behind Khalil and trembling with fear. But what could fear do to the heart of a woman who found Truth and followed him? What could the scorn of the crowd do to the soul of a maiden who had been awakened by Love? Sheik Abbas looked at the young man, and with a thundering voice he interrogated him saying, "What is your name, man?" "Khalil is my name," answered the youth. The Sheik returned, "Who are your father and mother and relatives, and where were you born?" Khalil turned toward the fellahin, who looked upon him with hateful eyes, and said, "The oppressed poor are my clan and my relatives, and this vast country is my birthplace."

Sheik Abbas, with an air of ridicule, said, "Those people whom you claim as kin demand that you be punished, and the country you assert as your birthplace objects to your being a member of its people." Khalil replied, "The ignorant nations arrest their good men and turn them into their despots; and a country, ruled by a tyrant, persecutes those who try to free the people from the yoke of slavery. But will a good son leave his mother if she is ill? Will a merciful man deny his brother who is miserable? Those poor men who arrested me and brought me here today are the same ones who surrendered their lives to you yesterday. And this vast earth that disapproves my existence is the one that does not yawn and swallow the greedy despots."

The Sheik uttered a loud laugh, as if wanting to depress the young man's spirit and prevent him from influencing the audience. He turned to Khalil and said impressively, "You cattle grazier, do you think that we will show more mercy than did the monks, who expelled you from the convent? Do you think that we feel pity for a dangerous agitator?" Khalil responded, "It is true that I was a cattle grazier, but I am glad that I was not a butcher. I led my herds to the rich pastures and never grazed them on arid land. I led my animals to pure springs and kept them from contaminated marshes. At eventide I brought them safely to their shed and never left them in the valleys as prey for the wolves. Thus I have treated the animals; and if you had pursued my course and treated human beings as I treated my flock, these poor people would not live in wretched huts and suffer the pangs of poverty, while you are living like Nero in this gorgeous mansion."

The Sheik's forehead glittered with drops of perspiration, and his smirk turned into anger, but he tried to show only calm by pretending that he did not heed Khalil's talk, and he expostulated, pointing at Khalil with his finger, "You are a heretic, and we shall not listen to your ridiculous talk; we summoned you to be tried as a criminal, and you realize that you are in the presence of the Lord of this village who is empowered to represent his Excellency Emir Ameen Shebab. You are standing before Father Elias, the representative of the Holy Church whose teachings you have opposed. Now, defend yourself, or kneel down before these people and we will pardon you and make you a cattle grazier, as you were in the convent." Khalil calmly returned, "A criminal is not to be tried by another criminal, as an atheist will not defend himself before sinners." And Khalil looked at the audience and spoke to them saying, "My brethren, the man whom you call the Lord of your fields, and to whom you have yielded thus long, has brought me to be tried before you in this edifice which he built upon the graves of your forefathers. And the man who became a pastor of your church through your faith, has come to judge me and help you to humiliate me and increase my sufferings. You have hurried to this place from every direction to see me suffer and hear me plead for mercy. You have left your huts in order to witness your pinioned son and brother. You have come to see the prey trembling between the paws of a ferocious beast. You came here tonight to view an infidel standing before the judges. I am the criminal and I am the heretic who has been expelled from the convent. The tempest brought me into your village. Listen to my protest, and do not be merciful, but be just, for mercy is bestowed upon the guilty criminal, while justice is all that an innocent man requires.

"I select you now as my jury, because the will of the people is the will of God. Awaken your hearts and listen carefully and then prosecute me according to the dictates of your conscience. You have been told that I am an infidel, but you have not been informed of what crime or sin I have committed. You have seen me tied like a thief, but you have not yet heard about my offenses, for wrongdoings are not revealed in this court, while punishment comes out like thunder. My crime, dear fellowmen, is my understanding of your plight, for I felt the weight of the irons which have been placed upon your necks. My sin is my heartfelt sorrows for your women; it is my sympathy for your children who suck life from your breast mixed with the shadow of death. I am one of you, and my forefathers lived in these valleys and died under the same yoke which is bending your heads now. I believe in God who listens to the call of your suffering souls, and I believe in the Book that makes all of us brothers before the face of heaven. I believe in the teachings that make us all equal, and that render us unpinioned upon this earth, the stepping place of the careful feet of God.

"As I was grazing my cows at the convent, and contemplating the sorrowful condition you tolerate, I heard a desperate cry coming from your miserable homes—a cry of oppressed souls—a cry of broken hearts which are locked in your bodies as slaves to the lord of these fields. As I looked, I found me in the convent and you in the fields, and I saw you as a flock of lambs following a wolf to the lair; and as I stopped in the middle of the road to aid the lambs, I cried for help and the wolf snapped me with his sharp teeth.

"I have sustained imprisonment, thirst, and hunger for the sake of Truth that hurts only the body. I have undergone suffering beyond endurance because I turned your sad sighs into a crying voice that rang and echoed in every corner of the convent. I never felt fear, and my heart never tired, for your painful cry was injecting a new strength into me every day, and my heart was healthy. You may ask yourself now saying, 'When did we ever cry for help, and who dares open his lips?' But I say unto you, your souls are crying every day, and pleading for help every night, but you cannot hear them, for the dying man cannot hear his own heart rattling, while those who are standing by his bedside can surely hear. The slaughtered bird, in spite of his will, dances painfully and unknowingly, but those who witness the dance know what caused at. In what hour of the day do you sigh painfully? Is it in the morning, when love of existence cries at you and tears the veil of slumber off your eyes and leads you like slaves into the fields? Is it at noon, when you wish to sit under a tree to protect yourself from the burning sun? Or at eventide, when you return home hungry, wishing for sustaining food instead of a meagre morsel and impure water? Or at night when fatigue throws you upon your rough bed, and as soon as slumber closes your eyes, you sit up with open eyes, fearing that the Sheik's voice is ringing in your ears?

"In what season of the year do you not lament yourselves? Is it in Spring, when nature puts on her beautiful dress and you go out to meet her with tattered raiment? Or in Summer, when you harvest the wheat and gather the sheaves of corn and fill the shelves of your master with the crop, and when the reckoning comes you receive naught but hay and tare? Is it in Autumn, when you pick the fruits and carry the grapes into the wine-press, and in reward for your toil you receive a jar of vinegar and a bushel of acorns? Or in Winter, when you are confined to your huts laden with snow, do you sit by the fire and tremble when the enraged sky urges you to escape from your weak minds?

"This is the life of the poor; this is the perpetual cry I hear. This is what makes my spirit revolt against the oppressors and despise their conduct. When I asked the monks to have mercy upon you, they thought that I was an atheist, and expulsion was my lot. Today I came here to share this miserable life with you, and to mix my tears with yours. Here I am now, in the grip of your worst enemy. Do you realize that this land you are working like slaves was taken from your fathers when the law was written on the sharp edge of the sword? The monks deceived your ancestors and took all their fields and vineyards when the religious rules were written on the lips of the priests. Which man or woman is not influenced by the lord of the fields to do according to the will of the priests? God said, 'With the sweat of thy brow, thou shall eat thy bread.' But Sheik Abbas is eating his bread baked in the years of your lives and drinking his wine mixed with your tears. Did God distinguish this man from the rest of you while in his mother's womb? Or is it your sin that made you his property? Jesus said, 'Gratis you have taken and gratis you shall give. . . . Do not possess gold, nor silver, neither copper.' Then what teachings allow the clergymen to sell their prayers for pieces of gold and silver? In the silence of the night you pray saying, 'Give us today our daily bread.' God has given you this land from which to draw your daily bread, but what authority has He given the monks to take this land and this bread away from you?

"You curse Judas because he sold his Master for a few pieces of silver, but you bless those who sell Him every day. Judas repented and hanged himself for his wrongdoing, but these priests walk proudly, dressed with beautiful robes, resplendent with shining crosses hanging over their chests. You teach your children to love Christ and at the same time you instruct them to obey those who oppose His teachings and violate His law.

"The apostles of Christ were stoned to death in order to revive in you the Holy Spirit, but the monks and the priests are killing that spirit in you so they may live on your pitiful bounty. What persuades you to live such a life in this universe, full of misery and oppression? What prompts you to kneel before that horrible idol which has been erected upon the bones of your fathers? What treasure are you reserving for your posterity?

"Your souls are in the grip of the priests, and your bodies are in the closing jaws of the rulers. What thing in life can you point at and say 'this is mine!' My fellowmen, do you know the priest you fear? He is a traitor who uses the Gospel as a threat to ransom your money...a hypocrite wearing a cross and using it as a sword to cut your veins...a wolf disguised in lambskin...a glutton who respects the tables more than the altars...a gold-hungry creature who follows the Denar to the farthest land...a cheat pilfering from widows and orphans. He is a queer being, with an eagle's beak, a tiger's clutches, a hyena's teeth and a viper's clothes. Take the Book away from him and tear his raiment off and pluck his beard and do whatever you wish unto him; then place in his hand one Denar, and he will forgive you smilingly.

"Slap his face and spit on him and step on his neck; then invite him to sit at your board. He will immediately forget and untie his belt and gladly fill his stomach with your food.

"Curse him and ridicule him; then send him a jar of wine or a basket of fruit. He will forgive you your sins. When he sees a woman, he turns his face, saying, 'Go from me, Oh, daughter of Babylon.' Then he whispers to himself saying, 'Marriage is better than coveting.' He sees the young men and women walking in the procession of Love, and he lifts his eyes toward heaven and says, 'Vanity of vanities, all is vanity.' And in his solitude he talks to himself saying, 'May the laws and traditions that deny me the joys of life, be abolished.'

"He preaches to the people saying, 'Judge not, lest ye be judged.' But he judges all those who abhor his deeds and sends them to hell before Death separates them from this life.

"When he talks he lifts his head toward heaven, but at the same time, his thoughts are crawling like snakes through your pockets.

"He addresses you as beloved children, but his heart is

empty of paternal love, and his lips never smile at a child, nor does he carry an infant between his arms.

"He tells you, while shaking his head, 'Let us keep away from earthly things, for life passes like a cloud.' But if you look thoroughly at him, you will find that he is gripping on to life, lamenting the passing of yesterday, condemning the speed of today, and waiting fearfully for tomorrow.

"He asks you for charity when he has plenty to give; if you grant his request, he will bless you publicly, and if you refuse him, he will curse you secretly.

"In the temple he asks you to help the needy, and about his house the needy are begging for bread, but he cannot see or hear.

"He sells his prayers, and he who does not buy is an infidel, excommunicated from Paradise.

"This is the creature of whom you are afraid. This is the monk who sucks your blood. This is the priest who makes the sign of the Cross with the right hand, and clutches your throat with the left hand.

"This is the pastor whom you appoint as your servant, but lie appoints himself as your master. This is the shadow that embraces your souls from birth until death.

"This is the man who came to judge me tonight because my spirit revolted against the enemies of Jesus the Nazarene Who loved all and called us brothers, and Who died on the Cross for us."

Khalil felt that there was understanding in the villagers' hearts; his voice brightened and he resumed his discourse saying, "Brethren, you know that Sheik Abbas has been appointed as Master of this village by Emir Shehab, the Sultan's representative and Governor of the Province, but I ask you if anyone has seen that power appoint the Sultan as the god of this country. That Power, my fellow men, cannot be seen, nor can you hear it talk, but you can feel its existence in the depths of your hearts. It is that Power which you worship and pray for every day saying, 'Our Father which art in heaven.' Yes, your Father Who is in heaven is the one Who appoints kings and princes, for He is powerful and above all. But do you think that your Father, Who loved you and showed you the right path through His prophets, desires for you to be oppressed? Do you believe that God, Who brings forth the rain from heaven, and the wheat from the hidden seeds in the heart of the earth, desires for you to be hungry in order that but one man will enjoy His bounty? Do you believe that the Eternal Spirit Who reveals to you the wife's love, the children's pity and the neighbor's mercy, would have upon you a tyrant to enslave you through your life? Do you believe that the Eternal Law that made life beautiful, would send you a man to deny you of that happiness and lead you into the dark dungeon of painful Death? Do you believe that your physical strength, provided you by nature, belongs beyond your body to the rich?

"You cannot believe in all these things, because if you do you will be denying the justice of God who made us all equal, and the light of Truth that shines upon all the peoples of the earth. What makes you struggle against yourselves, heart against body, and help those who enslave you while God has created you free on this earth?

"Are you doing yourselves justice when you lift your eyes towards Almighty God and call him Father, and then turn around, bow your heads before a man, and call him Master?

"Are you contented, as sons of God with being slaves of man? Did not Christ call you brethren? Yet Sheik Abbas calls you servants Did not Jesus make you free in Truth and Spirit? Yet the Emir made you slaves of shame and corruption

Did not Christ exalt you to heaven? Then why are you descending to hell? Did He not enlighten your hearts? Then why are you hiding your souls in darkness? God has placed a glowing torch in your hearts that glows in knowledge and beauty, and seeks the secrets of the days and nights; it is a sin to extinguish that torch and bury it in ashes. God has created your spirits with wings to fly in the spacious firmament of Love and Freedom; it is pitiful that you cut your wings with your own hands and suffer your spirits to crawl like insects upon the earth."

Sheik Abbas observed in dismay the attentiveness of the villagers, and attempted to interrupt, but Khalil, inspired, continued, "God has sown in your hearts the seeds of Happiness; it is a crime that you dig those seeds out and throw them willfully on the rocks so the wind will scatter them and the birds will pick them. God has given you children to rear, to teach them the truth and fill their hearts with the most precious things of existence. He wants you to bequeath upon them the joy of Life and the bounty of Life; why are they now strangers to their place of birth and cold creatures before the face of the Sun? A father who makes his son a slave is the father who gives his child a stone when he asks for bread. Have you not seen the birds of the sky training their young ones to fly? Why, then, do you teach your children to drag the shackles of slavery? Have you not seen the flowers of the valleys deposit their seeds in the sun-heated earth? Then why do you commit your children to the cold darkness?"

Silence prevailed for a moment, and it seemed as if Khalil's mind were crowded with pain. But now with a low and compelling voice he continued, "The words which I utter tonight are the same expressions that caused my expulsion from the convent. If the lord of your fields and the pastor of your church were to prey upon me and kill me tonight, I will die happy and in peace because I have fulfilled my mission and revealed to you the Truth which demons consider a crime. I have now completed the will of Almighty God."

There had been a magic message in Khalil's voice that forced the villagers' interest. The women were moved by the sweetness of his words and looked upon him as a messenger of peace, and their eyes were rich with tears.

Sheik Abbas and Father Elias were shaking with anger. As Khalil finished, he walked a few steps and stopped near Rachel and Miriam. Silence dominated the courtroom, and it seemed as if Khalil's spirit hovered in that vast hall and diverted the souls of the multitude from fearing Sheik Abbas and Father Elias, who sat trembling in annoyance and guilt.

The Sheik stood suddenly and his face was pale. He looked toward the men who were standing about him as he said, "What has become of you, dogs? Have your hearts been poisoned? Has your blood stopped running and weakened you so that you cannot leap upon this criminal and cut him to pieces? What awful thing has he done to you?" Having finished reprimanding the men, he raised a sword and started toward the fettered youth, whereupon a strong villager walked to him, gripped his hand and said, "Lay down your weapon, Master, for he who draws the sword to kill, shall, by the sword, be killed!"

The Sheik trembled visibly and the sword fell from his hand. He addressed the man saying, "Will a weak servant oppose his Master and benefactor?" And the man responded, "The faithful servant does not share his Master in the committing of crimes; this young man has spoken naught but the truth." Another man stepped forward and assured, "This man is innocent and is worthy of honor and respect." And a woman raised her voice saying, "He did not swear at God or curse any saint; why do you call him heretic?" And Rachel asked, "What is his crime?" The Sheik shouted, "You are rebellious, you miserable widow; have you forgotten the fate of your husband who turned rebel six years ago?" Upon hearing these impulsive words, Rachel shivered with painful anger, for she had found the murderer of her husband. She choked her tears and looked upon the throng and cried out, "Here is the criminal you have been trying for six years to find; you hear him now confessing his guilt. He is the killer who has been hiding his crime. Look at him and read his face; study him well and observe his fright; he shivers like the last leaf on winter's tree. God has shown you that the Master whom you have always feared is a murderous criminal. He caused me to be a widow amongst these women, and my daughter an orphan amidst these children." Rachel's utterance fell like thunder upon the Sheik's head, and the uproar of men and exaltation of women fell like firebrands upon him.

The priest assisted the Sheik to his seat. Then he called the servants and ordered them saying, "Arrest this woman who has falsely accused your Master of killing her husband; drag her and this young man into a dark prison, and any who oppose you will be criminals, excommunicated as he was from the Holy Church." The servants gave no heed to his command, but remained motionless staring at Khalil who was still bound with rope. Rachel stood at his right and Miriam at his left like a pair of wings ready to soar aloft into the spacious sky of Freedom.

His beard shaking with anger, Father Elias said, "Are you denying your Master for the sake of an infidel criminal and a shameless adulteress?" And the oldest one of the servants answered him saying, "We have served Sheik Abbas long for bread and shelter, but we have never been his slaves." Having thus spoken, the servant took off his cloak and turban and threw them before the Sheik and added, "I shall no longer require this raiment, nor do I wish my soul to suffer in the narrow house of a criminal." And all the servants did likewise and Joined the crowd whose faces radiated with joy, symbol of Freedom and Truth. Father Elias finally saw that his authority had declined, and he left the place cursing the hour that brought Khalil to the village. A strong man strode to Khalil and untied his hands, looked at Sheik Abbas who fell like a corpse upon his seat, and boldly addressed him saying, "This fettered youth, whom you have brought here tonight to be tried as a criminal, has lifted our depressed spirits and enlightened our hearts with Truth and Knowledge. And this poor widow whom Father Elias referred to as a false accuser has revealed to us the crime you committed six years past. We came here tonight to witness the trial of an innocent youth and a noble soul. Now, heaven has opened our eyes and has shown us your atrocity; we shall leave you and ignore you and allow heaven to do its will."

Many voices were raised in that hall, and one could hear a certain man saying, "Let us leave this ill-famed residence for our homes." And another one remarking, "Let us follow this young man to Rachel's home and listen to his wise sayings and consoling wisdom." And a third one saying, "Let us seek his advice, for he knows our needs." And a fourth one calling out, "If we are seeking justice, let us complain to the Emir and tell him of Abbas' crime." And many were saying, "Let us petition the Emir to appoint Khalil as our Master and ruler, and tell the Bishop that Father Elias was a partner in these crimes." While the voices were rising and falling upon the Sheik's ears like sharp arrows,

Khalil lifted his hands and calmed the villagers saying, "My brethren; do not seek haste, but rather listen and meditate. I ask you, in the name of my love and friendship for you, not to go to the Emir, for you will not find justice. Remember that a ferocious beast does not snap another one like him, neither should you go to the Bishop, for he knows well that the house cloven amid itself shall be ruined. Do not ask the Emir to appoint me as the Sheik in this village, for the faithful servant does not like to be an aid to the evil Master. If I deserve your kindness and love, let me live amongst you and share with you the happiness and sorrows of Life. Let me join hands and work with you at home and in the fields, for if I could not make myself one of you, I would be a hypocrite who does not live according to his sermon. And now, as the axe is laid unto the root of the tree, let us leave Sheik Abbas alone in the court room of his conscience and before the Supreme Court of God whose sun shines upon the innocent and the criminal."

Having thus spoken, he left the place, and the multitude followed him as if there were a divine power in him that attracted their hearts. The Sheik remained alone with the terrible silence, like a destroyed tower, suffering his defeat quietly, like a surrendering commander. When the multitude reached the church yard and the moon was just showing from behind the cloud, Khalil looked at them with the eyes of love like a good shepherd watching over his herd He was moved with sympathy upon those villagers who symbolized an oppressed nation; and he stood like a prophet who saw all the nations of the East walking in those valleys and dragging empty souls and heavy hearts.

He raised both hands toward heaven and said, "From the bottom of these depths we call thee, Oh, Liberty. Give heed to us! From behind the darkness we raise our hands to thee, Oh, Liberty. Look upon us! Upon the snow, we worship before thee, Oh, Liberty. Have mercy on us! Before thy great throne we stand, hanging on our bodies the blood-stained garments of our forefathers, covering our heads with the dust of the graves mixed with their remains, carrying the swords that stabbed their hearts, lifting the spears that pierced their bodies, dragging the chains that slowed their feet, uttering the cry that wounded their throats, lamenting and repeating the song of our failure that echoed throughout the prison, and repeating the prayers that came from the depths of our fathers' hearts. Listen to us, Oh Liberty, and hear us. From the Nile to the Euphrates comes the wailing of the suffering souls, in unison with the cry of the abyss; and from the end of the East to the mountains of Lebanon, hands are stretched to you, trembling with the presence of Death. From the shores of the sea to the end of the Desert, tear flooded eyes look beseechingly toward you. Come, Oh, Liberty, and save us.

"In the wretched huts standing in the shadow of poverty and oppression, they beat at their bosoms, soliciting thy mercy; watch us, oh Liberty, and have mercy on us. In the pathways and in the houses miserable youth calls thee; in the churches and the mosques, the forgotten Book turns to thee; in the courts and in the palaces the neglected Law appeals to thee. Have mercy on us, Oh Liberty, and save us. In our narrow streets the merchant sells his days in order to make tribute to the exploiting thieves of the West, and none would give him advice. In the barren fields the fellah tills the soil and sows the seeds of his heart and nourishes them with his tears, but he reaps naught except thorns, and none would teach him the true path. In our arid plains the Bedouin roams barefoot and hungry, but none would have mercy on him; speak, Oh Liberty, and teach us! Our sick lambs are grazing upon the grassless prairie, our calves are gnawing on the roots of the trees, and our horses are feeding on dry plants. Come, Oh Liberty, and help us. We have been living in darkness since the beginning, and like prisoners they take us from one prison to another, while time ridicules our plight. When will dawn come? Until when shall we bear the scorn of the ages? Many a stone have we been dragging, and many a yoke has been placed upon our necks. Until when shall we bear this human outrage? The Egyptian slavery, the Babylonian exile, the tyranny of Persia, the despotism of the Romans, and the greed of Europe...all these things we have suffered. Where are we going now, and when shall we reach the sublime end of the rough roadway? From the clutches of Pharaoh to the paws of Nebuchadnezzar, to the iron hands of Alexander, to the swords of Herod, to the talons of Nero, and the sharp teeth of Demon...into whose hands are we now to fall, and when will Death come and take us, so we may rest at last?

"With the strength of our arms we lifted the columns of the temple, and upon our backs we carried the mortar to build the great walls and the impregnable pyramids for the sake of glory. Until when shall we continue building such magnificent palaces and living in wretched huts? Until when shall we continue filling the bins of the rich with provisions, while sustaining weak life on dry morsels? Until when shall we continue weaving silk and wool for our lords and masters while we wear naught except tattered swaddles?

"Through their wickedness we were divided amongst ourselves; and the better to keep their thrones and be at ease, they armed the Druze to fight the Arab, and stirred up the Shiite to attack the Sunnite, and encouraged the Kurdish to butcher the Bedouin, and cheered the Mohammedan to dispute with the Christian. Until when shall a brother continue killing his own brother upon his mother's bosom? Until when shall the Cross be kept apart from the Crescent* before the eyes of God? Oh Liberty, hear us, and speak in behalf of but one individual, for a great fire is started with a small spark. Oh Liberty, awaken but one heart with the rustling of thy wings, for from one cloud alone comes the lightning which illuminates the pits of the valleys and the tops of the mountains. Disperse with thy power these black clouds and descend like thunder and destroy the thrones that were built upon the bones and skulls of our ancestors."

> "Hear us, Oh Liberty;
> Bring mercy, Oh Daughter of Athens;
> Rescue us, Oh Sister of Rome;
> Advise us, Oh Companion of Moses;
> Help us, Oh Beloved of Mohammed;
> Teach us, Oh Bride of Jesus;
> Strengthen our hearts so we may live,
> Or harden our enemies so we may perish
> And live in peace eternally."

As Khalil was pouring forth his sentiment before heaven, the villagers were gazing at him in reverence, and their love was springing forth in unison with the song of his voice until they felt that he became part of their hearts. After a short silence, Khalil brought his eyes upon the multitude and quietly said, "Night has brought us to the house of Sheik Abbas in order to realize the day light; oppression has arrested us before the cold Space, so we may understand one another and gather like chicks under the wings of the Eternal Spirit. Now let us go to our homes and sleep until we meet again tomorrow."

---

*The crescent is the emblem of the Mohammedan flag, flown over Syria during the Turkish rule. [Editor's note.]

Having thus spoken, he walked away, following Rachel and Miriam to their poor hovel. The throng departed and each went to his home, contemplating what he had seen and heard that memorable night. They felt that a burning torch of a new spirit had scoured their inner selves and led them into the right path. In an hour all the lamps were extinguished and Silence engulfed the whole village while Slumber carried the fellahin's souls into the world of strong dreams; but Sheik Abbas found no sleep all night, as he watched the phantoms of darkness and the horrible ghosts of his crimes in procession.

VIII

Two months had already passed and Khalil was still preaching and pouring his sentiments in the villagers' hearts, reminding them of their usurped rights and showing them the greed and oppression of the rulers and the monks. They listened to him with care, for he was a source of pleasure; his words fell upon their hearts like rain upon thirsty land. In their solitude, they repeated Khalil's sayings as they did their daily prayers. Father Elias commenced fawning upon them to regain their friendship; he became docile since the villagers found out that he was the Sheik's ally in crime, and the fellahin ignored him.

Sheik Abbas had a nervous suffering, and walked through his mansion like a caged tiger. He issued commands to his servants, but no one answered except the echo of his voice inside the marble walls. He shouted at his men, but no one came to his aid except his poor wife who suffered the pang of his cruelty as much as the villagers did. When Lent came and Heaven announced the coming of Spring, the days of the Sheik expired with the passing of Winter. He died after a long agony, and his soul was carried away on the carpet of his deeds to stand naked and shivering before that high Throne whose existence we feel, but cannot see. The fellahin heard various tales about the manner of Sheik Abbas' death; some of them related that the Sheik died insane, while others insisted that disappointment and despair drove him to death by his own hand. But the women who went to offer their sympathies to his wife reported that he died from fears because the ghost of Samaan Ramy hunted him and drove him every midnight out to the place where Rachel's husband was found slain six years before.

The month of Nisan proclaimed to the villagers the love secrets of Khalil and Miriam. They rejoiced the good tidings which assured them that Khalil would thereby remain in their village. As the news reached all the inhabitants of the huts, they congratulated one another upon Khalil's becoming their beloved neighbour.

When harvest time came, the fellahin went to the fields and gathered the sheaves of corn and bundles of wheat to the threshing floor. Sheik Abbas was not there to take the crop and have it carried to his bins. Each fellah harvested his own crop; the villagers' huts were filled with wheat and corn; their vessels were replenished with good wine and oil. Khalil shared with them their toils and happiness; he helped them in gathering the crop, pressing the grapes and picking the fruits. He never distinguished himself from any one of them except by his excess of love and ambition. Since that year and up to our present time, each fellah in that village commenced to reap with joy the crop which he sowed with toil and labour. The land which the fellahin tilled and the vineyards they cultivated became their own property.

Now, half a century has passed since this incident, and the Lebanese have awakened.

On his way to the Holy Cedars of Lebanon, a traveller's attention is caught by the beauty of that village, standing like a bride at the side of due valley. The wretched huts are now comfortable and happy homes surrounded by fertile fields and blooming orchards. If you ask any one of the residents about Sheik Abbas' history, he will answer you, pointing with his finger to a heap of demolished stones and destroyed walls saying, "This is the Sheik's palace, and this is the history of his life." And if you inquire about Khalil, he will raise his hand toward heaven saying, "There resides our beloved Khalil, whose life's history was written by God with glittering letters upon the pages of our hearts, and they cannot be effaced by the ages."

END